U. S. ROUTE 2 - CANADA TOO!

U. S. ROUTE 2 - CANADA TOO!

Robert Mac Kinnon

AuthorHouse™ LLC
1663 Liberty Drive
Bloomington, IN 47403
www.authorhouse.com
Phone: 1-800-839-8640

© 2014 Robert Mac Kinnon. All rights reserved.

No part of this book may be reproduced, stored in a retrieval system, or transmitted by any means without the written permission of the author.

Published by AuthorHouse   01/13/2014

ISBN: 978-1-4918-5275-0 (sc)
ISBN: 978-1-4918-5274-3 (e)

Library of Congress Control Number: 2014900868

Any people depicted in stock imagery provided by Thinkstock are models, and such images are being used for illustrative purposes only.
Certain stock imagery © Thinkstock.

This book is printed on acid-free paper.

Because of the dynamic nature of the Internet, any web addresses or links contained in this book may have changed since publication and may no longer be valid. The views expressed in this work are solely those of the author and do not necessarily reflect the views of the publisher, and the publisher hereby disclaims any responsibility for them.

Contents

ACKNOWLEDGEMENTS vii

INTRODUCTION ix

MAINE 1

NEW HAMPSHIRE 13

VERMONT 22

MONTREAL—QUEBEC 44

ONTARIO 55

MICHIGAN 75

WISCONSIN 88

MINNESOTA 96

NORTH DAKOTA 110

MONTANA 124

IDAHO 142

WASHINGTON 149

~ ACKNOWLEDGEMENTS ~

Simple honesty requires that I give credit where it is due: to the medical professionals of Northern Prince George's County, doctors, nurses, pharmacists, their staffs, personnel of Doctor's Community Hospital and especially the hard working crew of the emergency room. Thanks to all this good care, I was in condition to make the trip.

INTRODUCTION

Another time across the New Jersey Turnpike, but, this time it's different. It's the beginning of a full cross trip, and high time—as a matter of fact, and sad to say, It's well past the time I should have gone.

Way back, when we were both working, my wife and I followed this same route across the country, a section at a time. It took years. One time so far. Next time pick it up from where we left off and, again, go just so far. Section by section, vacation by vacation, trip after trip, and, after each, I would write about what we found, and research for the next trip. And, with respect, 9-11 and Katrina have virtually no part in any of this simply because they came later.

The original plan was to have the two of us make this trip after retirement. Her health wasn't up to it. Last year, after fifty-one years of marriage, she died. Her name was Theresa, Terry to those of us who loved her. Our family grief is, and will remain, private. So that's the last word you will see on this sad event.

Now, at age 77, I'm by myself and off to complete the whole route of the trip. To whatever extent it seems right to break out the difference between this and earlier trips, I will. Otherwise I'm going to carry on as though it was all the same trip, something like Thoreau writing as though his time at Walden Pond was one long uninterrupted stay. It wasn't.

So now I'm the white haired guy in the slow lane. It's more relaxing here, and even on the New Jersey Turnpike, there's some nice scenery. There are marshy areas that hint of how the ocean is just out of sight, the farms are still green, there's a touch of Autumn color in the trees, horses and cattle are still browsing in the warm open fields, and there was a man fishing from a rowboat in some stream that I crossed. Even the industrial areas look good. The buildings are clean and functional, and the grounds are well maintained and attractive.

It's good living conditions. The state has the gentle attractions of seashore and warm coastal plain, along with the employment attractions of strong vibrant industries. The poet, Walt Whitman, came here to convalesce and spent the twilight years of his life. Obviously, being sick, it wasn't a happy time, but he adjusted and did some fine late work here. Just watching the unfolding water, farm, and factory scenes makes me think that this is about as good a place as he could have been during those years. It's a good representative part of America, a land he called "Earth's modern wonder." That old poet spent his life celebrating everything American, our land, industry, history, diversity, and people—always the people. He was the singer for all America. And he ended his years in this gentle land.

Now I'm heading north to make my own cross country tour. Sometimes it's healthy to look beyond current events, to take time out to renew our acquaintance with our own land, and to get satisfaction and pride from seeing where we live and who we are. And that's all I'm going to do, look at the country, talk about the background and some of the people, be honest with my opinions, and open with my admiration and sentimentality. I don't have any unifying theories or answers to problems. I just think a celebration is in order.

Route 2 was selected because it's an old road and the routing includes parts of Canada, our friendly northern neighbor. The old roads, incidentally, are necessary to the plan. This New Jersey Turnpike is typical of the newer roads. They have controlled access, standardized services, and straight through driving with city bypasses. They're good for through driving and you'll see some scenery, but you'll never get to know either the country or the people.

The older roads were here for local use—between cities, through cities, to the farms, mines, resorts—before there were any interstate routes. The route numbers only came in 1926. It was a simple matter of the Federal Government mapping out the best cross country routes on the existing road network and assigning numbers. But Route 2 and most of the other old routes still have their original character. Each individual stretch of road is still local and, except for hiking, driving the old roads is still the best way to see America. So it's Route 2 with a connecting link through Canada. It's the land and stories I found along a thin slice of North America.

Before starting, though, let me offer a few particulars, just for background reasons. Terry and I grew up and got married in Boston, Massachusetts. Maryland was a career move, one that we never regretted. We had six children and nine grandchildren. After the children grew up, Terry worked in the University of Maryland's Admissions Office. I'm a retired Federal Civil Servant; most of my service was with The General Services Administration in Washington, D.C. When out on the road, I try to get out once a week, in clean jacket and slacks, to a nice sit down restaurant. And, one final peculiarity, I give names to my cars; the one I'm driving now is called Artemus.

MAINE

GETTING THERE

In two days I had been through six states, all with turnpikes. Driving gets to be a chore instead of a pleasure. On the third day I was faced with Maine's, the longest of the turnpikes, and a full day's drive that can only be measured by a dreary progression of miles and mile markers. Traffic reduces the road to an endurance contest. Speed reduces the land to a dull monotony. The only saving feature of turnpikes is that you get where you are going.

Houlton, Aroostook County

Ever since way back when I've admired Houlton. It's a great place to start this trip. Outside of the immediate center of town they have the usual variety of fast food places and other such familiar sights. But the buildings in Market Square, a few streets around the square, and here and there around town are old and interesting. On Green Street, which is a short ride from downtown, there's the weathered old Grange Building which is a classic. The downtown Court House is an impressive sight and, on Main Street, one building is dated 1912, while another is from 1929, the year of my birth. They're holding up well. Those old buildings are well kept and being used. It isn't touristy; it's authentic.

The difference this time around is that there is a sign announcing that Market Square has been designated a "Historic District." The century old look of this downtown area is natural, relaxed, enduring and endearing, and this is more than just my opinion. The designation makes it official. I didn't plan it this way, but it's nice to know that I'm starting this trip in a place that's certified Americana.

Just a few words on the overall area. Aroostook County is well kept and one of the richest farming areas in the United States. Unlike so many other parts of New England, the glaciers left rich soil deposits here, and the rainfall record is reliable and bountiful. The drawbacks are a short growing season and the distance from market.

Houlton to Bangor

This land was originally claimed by both the British and the French. Kings in both countries blithely gave grants to favorite subjects and the grants overlapped from Philadelphia to someplace north of Nova Scotia.

After the Revolution the British tried to claim this land all the way to the Penobscot River. They wanted all of northern Maine and here's the argument they used. Great Britain was still the inheritor of the French lands in North America, the French claim was through to the Penobscot River and, therefore, Britain had to defend the claim. That, of course, didn't work. The American negotiators pointed out that the United States was still defending the patent originally given by a British king, and this should take precedence over any grant given by a French monarch.

Different subject: the young Theodore Roosevelt was sent up here for his health. I don't know where he stayed but, wherever it was, it worked. He got back his good health and strength.

So long as I'm at it I might as well go on with some more old history and something else I couldn't find. What am I looking for? Big old white pine trees, and the reason I'm not finding them is because they're not here. This, however, does not stop me from looking.

There's a lot of forest. I found young white pine trees, and I found various pull over places with impressive views of the Penobscot River. But I didn't find any old white pine trees, the kind that are over two hundred feet tall. They're gone. Maybe there are some left on a far hill, in the deep woods—somewhere, but not along Route 2

Otherwise, though, the forests look just fine. My interest in the big trees is because they're important in American history, and Bangor is the center of this bit of history. The story goes back to old King George of Revolutionary war fame. He said tall white pine trees were a strategic reserve and, therefore, the property of the British government. They could only be cut when needed by His Majesty's Navy for ship masts. The King's agents were insistent on this, and it became one of the Revolutionary grievances. Colonists were determined to cut the trees for their lumber value. Even after the Revolution, though, the dispute wasn't really settled, at least not up here. This was one of those isolated areas where the British didn't really pull out. There were continuing territorial disputes up here until after the War of 1812. It wasn't until then that the British got out. After that, with the land secure and shipping lanes open, the forest became open to business.

Bangor

Once started, it didn't take Bangor long to overtake and pass all competition. The Penobscot River has an immense forested watershed. This is the birth place of our modern American lumber business. Bangor was the lumberjack starting point. The business, cutting, and floating practices grew up here, and Bangor crews set the pattern for all northern lumber operations. It took over a hundred years but, starting from here, the crews succeeded in cutting virtually every tall white pine tree through to the end of the forest in Minnesota.

Back in the peak years, the 1860s, the stretch of river from the coast to Bangor was the busiest waterway in the United States. There were sawmills along both banks, and hundreds of ships came from here and abroad for the choice lumber. Every year, when the ice melted, the city became an exciting, wild and wicked boom town. The lumbermen worked their way downstream, the sailors worked their way upstream, and they met in good old Bangor.

Bangor's a different place now, grown up, middle class, and respectable. The excitement's gone, even from the waterfront. There's a pristine new river walk, natural but no hint of past history. The petroleum storage tank areas are protected by high fences with barbed wire on top. Looking through the fence openings I saw a few crumbling ruins, not enough for any kind of a fair glimpse of the old vitality that used to dominate the river. Lumbermen, sailors, ship builders, mill workers, provisioners, ice-cutters, preachers, crooks, whores, drunks,—the whole exciting crowd—I hope someday they'll be remembered somewhere along the river. But that's enough of what I didn't find and what's gone.

Anyway, sometimes things from the past can stop you from seeing what's still around. It's like the museum at the entrance of the Penobscot Indian Nation. "Nation" incidentally is only a term for legal purposes. Actually we're talking about a pleasant modern suburb on a pretty big river island. It's populated by a people whose ancestors were reluctant to give up the Penobscot Valley, and they were brave enough to defend their land for a long time. Even the arch critic, Francis Parkman, gave them credit for that—not that he had much choice. The Penobscots chased the English out of the area three times in the olds French and Indian Wars. But that's the past and the museum does a good job of filling in the details.

Anyone taking time to drive beyond the museum will find a place with well kept grounds, a variety of home styles, a couple of churches, and the usual civic amenities. The Nation's here and now. It's doing well and it will continue to do well. On top of everything else, it won a long overdue out of court settlement from the Federal Government, and it invested the money wisely. What I see here is a normal settled neighborhood, a place where people know how to make the best of things and plan for the future. It has roots in the past, but they're pretty well buried. It's typical Bangor.

Like its Indian suburb, the city has the air of a settled comfortable place. The modern highways and airport have taken over the traffic, and that's probably why they've turned their back on the river. Everything's moved to the modern and convenient downtown, which is away from the river. Maybe there's more respectability and stability downtown. The move doesn't seem to have hurt business. Bangor's still the northland's center for financing, supplies, and social life. People come from as far as Canada for the amenities, shopping, and medical services. And, as I was reminded at dinner, everything's settled down to a more easy going place.

Business was off at the restaurant and the waiter spent some time gabbing with me. He didn't know anything about the old lumber and sailing days. Those things don't interest him at all. He's a bright enough fellow though, in his early thirties and originally from New York City. He and his girlfriend liked Nova Scotia best, but the Canadian authorities wouldn't let him stay because he didn't have a work permit. He thinks Bangor is the next best place to live. He can get by without too much effort, the people are friendly, and, because it's a small city with a relaxed pace, he doesn't feel the pressure or tensions.

I see his point. Bangor is a good second choice. It has its own quiet charm, especially in the downtown area, but its not a showplace. It's a place where people live, work, and relax. There's good shopping, a choice of restaurants, nightclubs, and a symphony orchestra. The state university is just outside the city, and both mountains and seashore are within a short drive. And, when the city gets around to it, something will be done to own up to some history in the riverfront area. In the meantime, as the waiter said, people don't feel the pressure or tensions.

Skowhegan, Benedict Arnold and the Quebec Campaign

For a town that has less then ten thousand people, Skowhegan plays a surprisingly big role in New England's history and tourist business. Located by one of the falls of the Kennebec River, it is a central Maine town with a crossroads location, a friendly downtown Chamber of Commerce building, and a large free parking lot.

Visitors can park and walk to and around the world's largest wooden Indian statue, the whole downtown area, and the historic island in the middle of the river. It's easy walking and the whole place is just as interesting and friendly as can be.

That's it for the tourist business, and I do want to get to a history story. Before getting to that, however, I have to take a minute to pay respects. It would be wrong to visit here and not honor the memory of Margaret Chase Smith, the stylish, bright, and witty United States Senator who charmed America with her integrity, determination, and down home common sense. Her trademark was the rose she always wore, and it wound up as one of the small but sweet stories of our time. On the first day that the Senate was back in session after assassination of President Kennedy, many Senators rose to say kind words of praise for our fallen leader. Margaret Chase Smith didn't say a word—she walked across to the Democratic side of the aisle, to what had once been John F. Kennedy's desk, took the rose off her lapel, and laid it on the desk.

I met one older woman who knew the Senator as "Maggie. I admired her house on the hill and spent some time in the connecting library. The exhibits do a fine job of highlighting her career and the events of the last century. It's a good place for scholars and students, and a fitting tribute for one who did so much for her state and the nation I'm satisfied. Now it's back to the island that's right in the downtown area so we can pick up on Benedict Arnold's campaign.

There's been historic controversy on the details of this campaign. Most of it goes back to the 1830s. A fellow named Codman wrote a popular book on the campaign. Then a fellow named Smith wrote a scholarly book in which he ridiculed Codman's version. Finally, in 1938, Kenneth Roberts performed a great service to the American public by gathering and printing copies of the available diaries and reminiscences of those who were in the campaign. Smith and the Roberts compilation are the reliable sources. Codman is not.

The historic signs are a mixed bag too. There's a sign at the back of a Skowhegan parking lot saying the Arnold camped on Skowhegan Island. This is misleading. Actually, he went on to Norridgewock where he spent the night in some widow's house. But other markers, especially the ones north of here on Route 201, do a first rate job of telling the story and detailing the route. For present purposes, though, Skowhegan's river island is the best place to start the story. There are two monuments in the quiet little park by the big white church. They speak of the courage of our troops in this early Revolutionary War campaign.

Those must have been heady days: correspondence committees, a Congress of the colonies, His Majesty's troops chased back from Lexington, Patrick Henry making that fiery speech in Virginia, the British army bottled up in Boston, and revolution against old England. Patriots were aflame with the rights of the common man and the ideas of liberty. There was no limit to revolutionary ambition and enthusiasm. For a time it seemed we should even be able to win over the old French stronghold in Quebec.

The invasion to win over Quebec was daring, but it was not an impractical campaign. American merchants in Montreal were busy spreading the message of liberty. An effective show of force might win some popular support from the French Canadian people. With a bold thrust through the woods we could reach Quebec before British reinforcements arrived. England would be deprived of this major northern stronghold. The wall of resistance would stretch from the St. Lawrence to Georgia. It was worth a try.

The problems were routing and weather. The troops were assembled around Boston but, except for some limited coastal operations, the British controlled the sea. The invasion would have to be by land. General Montgomery was in the Champlain Valley with a small American army and he would invade by way of Montreal. But that was at the opposite end of New England and it would take too long to have the troops from Boston join Montgomery. The only solution was to proceed directly and have Arnold and Montgomery join forces at Quebec City.

Arnold came up with the idea of following the old French missionary trail, an inland route that followed rivers and lakes through Maine to Quebec. It was a logical choice. The missionaries traveled it. The old Boston to Quebec stagecoach route was completed through this same area about forty years after Arnold's march. Now the State routes pretty well follow Arnold's route but not on a straight line. Actually, the route is roughly on two roads, with a mountain in between, and no connecting road over the mountain. Anyone wanting to follow the route can drive thirty five miles up Route 201 and find the historical marker for where Arnold left the river. After this, though, you'll have to double back and then go north on State Route 27.

The problem is that this isn't a natural route. There isn't any natural route between here and Quebec. Even today, except for those historic roads that have been forced through, Maine is still uninhabited and roadless in most of the area between here and Quebec.

Just wandering around on Skowhegan's river island, you can see some of the difficulty. Even with an electric company dam holding back some of the flow, the water at the bottom of the cliff is still rough and turbulent. Arnold came through in October, and it took several days just to get by here. The boats and supplies had to be hauled out of the river with rough pulleys, and then portaged to the other side of the falls. And, beyond here, it was all cold weather traveling and rough wilderness.

The missionaries made it, but they were single individuals traveling in good weather and traveling light. A force of rangers could navigate this country. But rangers were raiders and, if Quebec was to be taken and held, an army was required.

Army travel through this country, however, wasn't advisable, especially at this time of the year. The ruggedness of the terrain and the impossibility of maintaining supply support through the wilderness area should have discouraged Arnold. The army could have turned back without shame. In fact, two of the militia companies, after voting on the matter, did turn back and there was no shame. But Arnold was full of fire and ambition; he wouldn't consider accepting defeat from the elements. At that time he was a bold and dashing American field commander, and he had the ability to inspire troops to superhuman efforts. They went on.

Despite the two lost militia companies, the bulk of the army was still New England militiamen, those brave and inexperienced citizen soldiers with old fashioned muskets who made u p so much of this country's Revolutionary War effort. There were also some professional types. General Washington provided three crack rifle companies. Two of them were from Pennsylvania. The third, which was from Virginia, was commanded by the fierce Daniel Morgan, who went on to become a legendary hero of the American Revolution. The Continental Army didn't have much to spare from the siege of Boston, but Washington wanted Quebec and he provided the best he could for this little army. The soldiers repaid with courage and their lives.

The elements didn't favor the march, and this ill fated little army suffered hardships and a high death rate on the long trek through Maine. They persisted through hills, swamps, rivers, unexpected rapids that overturned boats, rain, cold, snow, dysentery, and a flood that destroyed supplies. When the food ran out they ate the oxen and then the dogs. All told it took eight weeks but, with a considerably reduced, sick, hungry, and weary army, Arnold made it to Quebec. And General Montgomery joined him there.

The French Canadians understood what was going on, and the habitants, the common people to whom the revolution was supposed to be attractive, sympathized with the Americans. Arnold's weary and sick troops were nursed back to health by these kind country people. However, with some exceptions which were mostly in the Montreal area, the French Canadians didn't provide support for the American cause. And it's sad to know that Arnold gave the British a list of these pro-American Canadians. But that was later. The problem here was that the hoped for French Canadian support didn't materialize.

The British administrators of Quebec had respected French property customs and the status of the Catholic Church. The conservative powers—landowners and Catholic clergy—were convinced that there would be more safety and stability in continued British rule. The common people, the habitants, understood the attraction of the revolutionary appeals but, beyond this, they didn't have enough in common with the rebelling colonists. They weren't convinced that they belonged in an American freedom movement. The Quebec French stayed neutral.

Montgomery and Arnold were on their own, in an alien land, with a position that was bad and getting worse. They were outnumbered, ammunition was low, supply funds were exhausted, and the militia terms of service were due to run out. They gambled on a surprise attack.

With a combined force of about a thousand men, they attacked Quebec at night and under cover of a snowstorm, on December 31, 1775. General Montgomery was killed and, in his quarter, the American attack was stopped. Arnold, who was attacking from a different side of the city, was severely wounded but his troops broke through the defenses and entered the city of Quebec. If both groups had succeeded and combined in the city, Quebec would probably have been taken. As it turned out, Arnold's troops were in an untenable position and the forward element, which included Daniel Morgan and his Virginians, was cut off and captured. The majority of the troops, however, succeeded in getting out of the city and back to their own American camp.

There was defeat, but no lack of courage. This group never lacked courage. And Arnold, even when he was on our side, had a raging devil in him. Still, it was defeat and, when the British reinforcements arrived, a forced retreat. The American army held together as it retreated through Montreal and down the Champlain Valley into

New York, and they used every delaying tactic available to slow the British advance. Finally, Arnold and the tattered remains of his army, joined the American force that defeated General Burgoyne's British army at Saratoga, New York. It's interesting to know too that Daniel Morgan was back in duty at Saratoga. He had been freed on a prisoner exchange, and he came back to battle with a new force of riflemen. But these are consolations from a later campaign.

The sad fact is that the incredibly brave little army that completed the difficult portage around these falls in Skowhegan went on to suffering and defeat. New England men, Pennsylvanians, and Virginians tried to carry their revolution to Canada. They tried for a unified North America, and they paid the price for failure. They came surprisingly close, but they didn't change the course of history. The attack on Quebec failed, Canada remained British, and our army suffered a terrible mortality rate. They were brave men, though, and the Skowhegan monuments remind us that they never lost courage.

South Waterford and Charles F. "Artemus Ward" Brown

I'm off on a day trip to South Waterford, a little town about twenty miles below Route 2. It's a nice ride through two-lane rural Maine, a place where a general store/post office is still the social and business center for a community. And, at the end of the drive, I paid my respects at the grave of Charles F. Brown, the early American humorist who wrote the Attemus Ward letters.

Artemus Ward never really existed, at least not the one we're concerned with. To keep the story straight, though, there actually was a man with the name Artemus Ward. He was from an earlier time and he had his own claim to respectful memory. He was a general, a veteran from the French and Indian Wars who got out of his sick bed at the time of the American Revolution to take command of the troops around Boston. He was in charge until George Washington arrived as the new commander-in-chief. Then the real Artemus stayed on as second in command. Respects General.

But the Artemus who never really existed is an entirely different fellow. Brown dreamed him up, and Brown thought there was something funny about the name. Some people thought Brown's use of the name was disrespectful. Most people thought "so what" because Brown was so funny. I can't join in on any criticism, not after taking the same name for my car. I'm a fan of the character that Brown created. To add to that, I also like the way the name is sounded up here. The "e" in the middle is almost lost. With a New England accent it comes out AH-Te-MUS. Then, because this is rural northern New England, you kind of swallow the whole thing as you are saying it. How these people can talk this way, and still talk slow, is beyond me. But they do it, and when they do it with a name like Artemus, the sound is as brisk and sharp as a drum roll.

Sounds like I'm back again to something that sounds military. I can't seem to get away from the fact that the name belonged to a real general first. And I don't know why Brown didn't use his own name. It turned out to be good enough for the Peanut comic strip character, Charlie Brown. Was little Charlie really named after this early American humorist? Another thing I don't know, but I suspect he was. There's something intentional about every character in that comic strip. Anyway, it all works out to names or plots can be funny or not depending on who is putting the package together.

It takes talent. Imagine having just about every household in America turning pages every morning to find a dog who sits on top of his doghouse and pretends to be a World War I ace. It's preposterous and we love it. There's a whole distorted mirror world in that comic strip. We see it and we laugh at ourselves. And our ancestors waited for the next Artemus Ward letter so they could enjoy their laugh.

Artemus was a likeable scoundrel who owned a traveling show that included wax statues, animals, and an occasional fake freak—admission only fifteen cents. As proud owner of this unlikely show, he wrote preposterous letters about adventures with famous people, temperance lecturers, strange females, opera singers, swindlers, and other assorted characters. Personally, Artemus, who was accommodating in matters of religion and politics, tried to avoid trouble; he just couldn't avoid giving advice.

Sometimes the advice was silly. The Prince of Wales was advised, on the occasion of his wedding, that now he could eat onions. In what passed for humor in those days,. Artemus advised President Lincoln to fill his cabinet with showmen because they have neither politics nor principles, but thy know how to please the public. In another place we find a prisoner blaming his parents for not giving him a better education: if he were better schooled he could have been a successful white collar crook instead of a petty thief and prisoner.

Artemus carried on in country bumpkin dialect, things like, *"It is easy enough to see why a man goes to the poor house or the penitentiary. It is becawz he can't help it. But why he should woluntarily go and life in Washinton is entirely beyond my comprehension."* It was good broad American folk humor, robust, witty, presumptuous, understanding, sly, cornball, and, sorry to say, dated. Oh well, a hundred and fifty years from now people will wonder why we laughed at that silly dog and those strange little children.

Another thing I'm sorry to say, Brown's career was cut short. He died from tuberculosis at age thirty three. He was well liked and a decent sort of fellow, though, and it's amazing to consider all he did accomplish in such a short life. On top of everything else, he gets credit for giving a helping hand to a new young comic, Samuel Clemens, who wrote under the name Mark Twain. After that, of course, Twain went on to greater fame. But, in his own time, Brown was the most popular comic in America. Even President Lincoln was one of his fans. As a matter of fact, Lincoln actually read the latest Artemus Ward letter to his cabinet before reading them the Emancipation Proclamation.

Now this gifted and decent author lies in a modest family burial plot in a peaceful little cemetery at the edge of his home town of South Waterford, Maine. It's a pleasant final resting place. There's a new section below here, a meadow across the street, trees all around, and the gravestone says "His memory will live as a sweet and unfading recollection."

Respects and rest in peace Charles F. "Artemus Ward" Brown. Some of us still read your work. And there's a strange little comic strip kid with your name. He's too young to have a traveling show, but he has a mixed up baseball team, and he's usually good for a morning laugh.

NEW HAMPSHIRE

Northern New England and the White Mountains

We're on different time schedules, but, from what I can follow, Mount Washington and I are both visitors to this part of the world. This mountain, along with the rest of the Appalachian mountain chain, was built up way back when there wasn't any North America. Different continents or land masses or something were grinding against each other in some far distant part of the world. Local books talk about the mountains being pushed up by compressive pressure from the east, but that doesn't mean we can look for anything in the Atlantic Ocean. I'm not sure it even means the east; it just means that now the facing is to the east. Judging by some old Department of the Interior reconstructions, I would guess the push came from something that's now part of North Africa. The continents were stuck together then. But there was a rift or rifts that broke up the old super continent, and Mount Washington, along with the rest of New Hampshire's White Mountains, spent a couple of hundred million years or so moving north so they could be here to do their part in this grand Fall season.

There's more than enough off-trail wilderness in these areas for those who want it. The writings of Henry David Thoreau are still a good read if you're interested in Maine's Mount Kathadin. The better story in the White Mountains is Hawthorne and his more genteel love of nature. Either place, though, and either choice, you have to leave the trail. Count me out.

I wouldn't be here if they didn't have good roads, modern tourist facilities, and convenient restaurants. My enjoyment of the White Mountains, all of northern New England in fact, is from the car window, some scenic overlooks, a few convenient tourist trails, and a little of my own poking around in the more settled lowland regions. It's enough. It has to be. Besides, at this stage of life I find myself taking more interest in the history of the land. It's not complete, but scientists have made amazing progress.

It's only about a hundred and fifty years ago that Professor Agassiz of Harvard was trying to convince people that America had a recent ice age, and Professor Dana of Yale was trying to reconcile the expanding time frames of geologic history with the Book of Genesis. New information was being developed, new theories were being advanced, and, as usual, there was a need to placate conservative resistance. But the scientific evidence became overwhelming, and it became more acceptable as people came to realize that there were practical applications. The railroads, the mining industries, and the developing states of the west needed geological surveys. Now we're mixing earth and space studies, getting ever more exotic findings, and making better frying pans. Anyway, and despite the emphasis on practical applications, the new sciences have given us a better understanding and appreciation of the history of the land.

These are old mountains, dating back to some hundreds of millions of years ago. They're part of the Appalachian chain, but each part of the chain had its own local building material. And each part of the chain has its own erosion history. Two hundred million years of being worn down by local weather and environmental conditions. Vermont had more shale and the mountains have been reduced to high hills. The towering White and Kathadin mountains have more granite, and there are slopes that may have been parts of even older mountains. Various upland areas have been covered by lakes that no longer exist. Rain and wind are the most persistent erosion forces. They're slow but they do the job. For a practical illustration of their effectiveness visit an old cemetery and see the erosion of the writing on the gravestones. But most of all, here in New England, its been the glaciers.

Professor Agassiz was right. Glacial ice covered large areas of Canada and northern parts of the United States four time in the past million years. Whether these ice ages were caused by fluctuations in the sun's output, tilting of the poles, other variations in the earth's orbit, changes in ocean currents, atmospheric gas balls, or some other reason, isn't known. But it's good to know our scientists are busy working out the answers. Our descendants might need them. It's less than twenty thousand years since the last of the glaciers retreated from these parts, and there's reason to believe they'll be back within the next ten thousand years of so. Geologically, these are short time spans. The glaciers were recent history.

So, in a general sort of way, it makes sense to say that everyone and everything is on a visitor's schedule, and scientists have the job of figuring out the time tables. The parts that have to do with hundreds of millions of years are too deep for me. They get into sophisticated dating processes, laser beams from space, high resolution photography, ocean floor mapping, and a lot of other things I can't pick up on as I ride around the country. I get by as best I can on Department of the Interior picture booklets and a few other easy sources. But the glaciers are a different story. I can see what happened.

These mountains were sculptured by the ice. The glaciers grew to such a mass that, for a while, they even covered Mount Washington. These were moving ice masses and they scraped, cut, pushed, carried, and redistributed. The weight and force was tremendous. The large hollows in the sides of the White and Kathadin mountains are glacial cirque bites, areas that were ground away by hundreds of years of pressure from moving ice and swirling water. The lakes, the wide valleys, the boulders strewn in odd places—they're all glacial after effects. There's some good valley farmland and, even in higher areas, there are some good flat stretches but, overall, farmland has been depleted. Much of what was pushed in front of the glaciers ended in the ocean. Much of what was left is rocky scrapings, the glacial till of New England.

The land is water rich and a scenic wonderland, but it can't support a large population. Except for Champlain, the major use for the lakes can only be recreational. The rivers are swift running and rock strewn—good for fishing and sometimes for floating logs, but not for transportation. There are gravel pits and granite quarries, but the area is poor in mineral resources. The hills are good for lumber and skiing, but not much else. The farms are scattered. There are a few cities, but its more a land of small towns with the local economy based on lumber, tourist trade, or agriculture. River towns are dominated by plants, usually woodworking or pulp. In the older valley towns the church is still the dominating feature.

I enjoy seeing the place on old roads that follow the natural contour of the land. The scenery is forever changing and, since the traffic is light, there's no problem with slowing down or stopping to admire different scenes. I see smaller towns and more wilderness on the side trips. The scenic vistas are better on Route 2. The road goes over hills, around hills, on the edge of farms, through forests, past lakes, along the side of rivers, and down the main streets of towns. And, except for the White Mountains, there's a classic balance that makes the area seem friendly and comfortable. The hills, rivers, meadows, and lakes seem to be proportioned to complement each other, and the towns and farms blend in as if they were a natural part of the scenery.

The White Mountains are different. They stood up to the glaciers. They're nature's show of strength—monumental, cold and aloof. They're famous for treacherous terrain, fierce storms, cold weather records, and wild grandeur. That's the combination that attracts artists and tourists, awesome beauty and the thrill of danger. Off-trail types come for the challenge and, so far as I can determine, they're not disappointed. I'm the other type. I keep to the trail, stay in line, and obey the signs. Even so, I enjoy it.

Mount Washington Hotel

Originally, I wanted to see the old Mount Washington Hotel because it's famous in economic history. It's the place where they held the Bretton Woods Conference, and set up the World Bank and the International Monetary Fund. Now I've come around to admiring the hotel just for itself. It looks like a stunning white fairy tale castle, big but beautifully proportioned, turrets, flags flying, porches, grand circular drive, golf, tennis, restaurants and lounges.

It's the grand old hotel in all its glory, the kind of place that became popular when the railroads were first built. The old folks, women, and children would season here while the men stayed home making money, and sometimes indulging in other pursuits. That was high society's idea of fashion and fun. Whose fun? That's an old argument. Anyway, the place was built to pamper rich people of another age. It's still here, beautifully kept, all the modern conveniences, and well worth the trip.

Another thing, there doesn't seem to be any problem with showing up and wandering around, even when you're not a paying guest. It's an open, almost a public place, with about half the first floor taken up by the gracious old type lobby. Crowds are coming and going all the time. There are stands, stores, a travel counter, seating areas, and, off to one side, a reservations desk. It's the kind of place that's comfortable and interesting, even for casual visitors. The windows are set up to give a grand view of the mountains. And, down one of the halls, there are some vintage pictures commemorating the Bretton Woods Conference.

It's ironic. The Conference is the hotel's claim to historic fame, yet, it's the one time it gave bad service. That was back in 1944, near the end of World War II. The hotel had been closed for three years, and expertise and staffing just weren't available to run a smooth operation for this one conference. With good size delegations from forty-four nations, the service was on a catch as catch can basis. Dean Acheson, who attended for the State Department, and had the good sense to make his own separate reservations at some small inn that was still in business, did an entertaining job of describing the confusion in his book, *Present at the Creation*. But it was only the hotel services that were erratic and confused. The conference was a success.

Harry Dexter White of the U.S. Treasury Department prepared the original proposals and organized the conference. He and Lord Keynes from Great Britain had worked for two years on the details for these proposed new organizations and, both being strong personalities, they dominated the proceedings. They were hard drivers. The work sessions lasted from twelve to fourteen hours a day but Keynes, although they tried to cover it up at the time, had a heart attack and had to cut back on his working hours.

White was chairing the group that established the International Monetary Fund, and he continued the pace. He was a brilliant man and, for a while, he was successful, but things didn't work out for him. Four years after this conference he died at his Summer home at Fitzwilliam, New Hampshire. There didn't seem to be any problem immediately after the conference. He was promoted to the position of Assistant Secretary of the Treasury and, a short while later, he became the first U.S. Executive Director of the International Monetary Fund. Everything seemed to be going fine. Then his reputation was challenged.

Charges were made in 1947 and 1948 that Harry White was a "Fellow Traveler" who supplied sensitive American Government documents to Russian intelligence agents. A 1947 Grand Jury didn't find any cause for indictment and, in the following year, at his own request, White testified before the House Un-American Activities Committee and gave a forceful and convincing defense of his loyalty and patriotism. Three days later he died of a heart attack. He was the highest government official to be accused of such a crime and, in the years following his death, the charges became more heated and political. Unfortunately, this controversy distracted attention from his real and substantial accomplishments. Personally, from what I've read, I believe Harry White was innocent but, other than shedding a tear for a fellow Civil Servant, I'm not going into that.

Harry's ending was sad but his Fund's a success. Part of the story, the part we're concerned with, is his choice of this location for the meetings. Forgetting the service problems, it's easy to understand the reasons. There's nothing like a grand old hotel for crowd control. The place was built to pamper and isolate those who could afford the best. It was a good place to coop up the world's financial leaders and drive them unmercifully, as he did, until they came to a workable agreement. Besides, as both Harry and the rich husbands knew, people are more likely to accept conditions when they're surrounded by beauty.

Lancaster and Old Stories

I can't remember where, but I read somewhere that the people in northern New England, more so than any other part of the United States, are of native stock, authentic Yankees, descendants of the original English settlers. And another lapse is that I can't find my original notes on this piece of Lancaster history. As memory serves it came from a newspaper article some twenty five or so years ago. A couple of local buffs remember the general outline of the story but none of us are in a position to research twenty-five year old newspaper files. However, I'm not giving up on this one; I'm going ahead with the story as picked up way back when.

Whoever it was did a nice job of writing Lancaster history, but they were stymied by the lack of historical records. It seems that, at one time, the town had two cannons that were captured from General Burgoyne's army. But the cannons are gone now. It's thought that one was sent to the State Capitol. The other one blew up when the townspeople tried to fire it as part of some old celebration. Sometimes it's tough to pin things down.

In Norridgewock, Maine, just a couple of days ago, I had to ask five people before I could get directions to an old French missionary grave. The lady in the little restaurant was a lot of fun and she kept kidding me because I never had corn chowder. She was obviously of Yankee stock, nevertheless, no, she had never heard of any French missionary around here. But she kept insisting I had to try her home made chowder and blueberry muffins. I agreed that the chowder was good and then we had some talk of children and how to make muffins.

That's how the trip goes. I start out looking for something significant and I get chowder and muffins. Maybe that's significant. I think a case could be made for that lady being representative of settler stock. Anyway, despite local disinterest, chowder, and muffins,—and case or no—I'm still concerned with the missing cannons and the French missionary's grave.

The priest, by the way, is dead because that good natured lady's ancestors shot him. His name was Sebastian Railes and he was encouraging the Indians to attack the English settlements.

Those sturdy and good natured ancestors had had enough. They were the victims of their own success and everybody else's policies. They didn't come to bring England's problems over here. They came to leave England behind and set up God-fearing and peaceful settlements in a new world. They succeeded, and they did it without stealing the land. In just about all the cases that can be checked, they occupied the land by treaty agreement or purchase. Yet, every time old England had a dispute with France, the hounds of Hell were loosed on the New England settlements.

Since then there have been many studies on the culture shock experienced by the Indian people. Today we see them as victims, and that's good. It shows that we've gained some understanding. However, as Francis Parkman once pointed out, this benevolent view of Indians "has never yet been held by any whose wives and children have lived in danger of his scalping knife."

These settlers were being brutally killed and, no matter whose foreign policy was involved, it became their war. They intended to capture Father Railes, but that doesn't matter. They would do whatever was necessary to stop the raids. And, with a tremendous outpouring of New England men, French Canada was defeated and eliminated as a threat.

Father Railes grave is marked by an old obelisk, and it's way back in a cemetery that's just north of the town. He was a good man and an effective missionary, but he died for a political cause. He's not considered among the Church's North American martyrs. Meanwhile the good natured lady goes on serving chowder and muffins and kidding people like me. I still think she's representative of settler stock.

The cannons, of course, were from a different war. Lancaster, New Hampshire, didn't even exist until just about at the end of the French and Indian Wars. For most of this time the nearest English outpost was about ninety miles down the river, at what's now the town of Charlestown. No one occupied these northern areas, not even the Indians. And no one knows why the Indians didn't live here. Maybe it was from fear of the Iroquois, their raids were the terror of the other tribes. Then again, it may have been the plague. Whatever the reason, this was the no man's land of the earlier wars.

That's why our Lancaster historian had his problems. Records weren't being kept. These people were just barely occupying the land when another invasion came from Canada. This time it was the British and Indians.

Everyone knew that one of King George's favorites, Johnny Burgoyne, was going to invade with a European army. And, by this time, the settlers were more American than British in their sentiments. They resented Great Britain's retention of authority to make rules on such things as taxes, trade, white pine trees, and further westward expansion. Nevertheless, Britain's biggest mistake was repeating French tactics. The settlers didn't respond until after a story had been spread about an outrageous killing of a white woman by Burgoyne's Indian allies.

Whatever the resentment of the moment, the call to arms was understood in its full import. It was revolution. So be it. Burgoyne's army was surrounded, defeated, and forced to surrender to an American army that was composed, in the main, of militia from the New England states.

Lancaster must have had some part in this. Otherwise they wouldn't have gotten those two cannons. If they were still available they'd make a nice addition on the green by the library, but that can never be. And here I'll complete the story and everyone can feel free to express their own sympathy—or satisfaction. The second cannon blew up when the town was celebrating the surrender of General Robert E. Lee.

VERMONT

New England Forests

I did my army tour in Europe after World War II and, like most GI's, I was amazed at the sight of the old world forests. Locals went through every part of those woods, picked up fallen branches, cut up fallen trees, and cleared the underbrush. Trees weren't cut, but everything else with any use was picked up as soon as it became available. None of this, of course, is good for wild life, which is probably why there wasn't any of it left, or at least not enough to make any difference. I did see a rabbit once but the poor thing looked lost with no place to hide. Anyway, with the animals gone, and the forest floors nice and clear, it does make for pleasant and safe walking. As a matter of fact, it's so open and tame I think Europeans have lost just about all sense of why their ancestors feared the woods. Snakes, bears, moose and other animals were part of it. Suspicions and fears of the unknown were other parts.

Time was when beautiful young maidens, nymphs as they were called, used to frolic and dance in the woods of old Europe. Even then, though, wise parents knew to keep their daughters home. Pan, part man part goat, did more than just pipe the dance tunes. He did a lusty job of chasing the nymphs. Then, if he failed to catch any, he would become nasty and go around scaring young girls and innocent travelers. This, by the way, is where we get the word panic. But even Pan seemed to hang around the edge of the woods, near where people lived. The deep woods were another and more scary story.

The Romans claimed that the Celts, who lived in the "All Gaul" of Julius Caesar fame, used to go to the deepest, coldest, and darkest parts of the forest to make hideous sacrifices, that there was so much blood and gore that even the birds and beasts would avoid these parts of the forest. Sounds like clever propaganda but, who knows, maybe the Romans were right about this. Still again, it is playing to the city dweller's in-built dread of people who live in the wild. However, to get on with this, both the Celts and Romans were afraid of the Germans who were coming from the even deeper dark northern forests, and all the while the Germans kept looking over their shoulders at the gloomy and fearsome forests that were still further north; they, too, were a driven people. But all this is old history, so old that it no longer seems to be a part of the European consciousness.

America was discovered, however, before Europe finished taming its own forests, at a time when people still had the old consciousness. The original settlers came here, ax in hand, and started cutting their way across a continent. You can still get some sense, up here, of how it might have looked shortly after the first landings.

In driving around you actually see clearings on some of the side roads. Some latter day pioneer gets a lot in the woods, gets rid of a few trees, clears some underbrush, and puts up a makeshift house or trailer. Nothing organized, just an occasional one here and there, usually with a vegetable garden. Nothing lasting either. But good luck to these forest dwellers. They're having their romance and, in a sense, they are doing the same thing as the original settlers. America was built from clearings.

A big difference, though is that most of the old timers didn't want to live that way. The latter day pioneers are moving here to be in the woods. The early settlers were trying to get rid of the woods, and they didn't have any romantic notions about trees. Even after the Indian threat was gone, pioneer wives dreamed of clearings in which there wouldn't be a single tree within falling distance of the house. And some of this attitude stayed around until the early 1900s. E. A. Robinson, Maine's prize winning poet, was probably in tune with local attitudes when he pictured trees as being hostile and gloomy. He could wax romantic about people, but definitely not about trees. In one poem he tells about a character named Old Archibald who gloats about how he cut the trees down because they were blocking his sunlight.

Gloat on Old Archibald. You had your day and enjoyed your sunlight. And your neighbors were just as indifferent as you on the matter of trees, and some of them were mighty careless. It wasn't as if anyone wanted those terrible fires back in the late 1800s. We know that. It was the careless use of fire. Despite the desolation, though, the trees have long since moved back and those areas are filled in now. Besides, the fires weren't the worst threat. No, the worst of it was the lumberjacks of your time, numbering in the thousands, who made the assault on these forests.

Man's greatest inroads were made in the middle of the nineteenth century by those tough old crews Bangor and other lumber centers. They went all through the deep woods, cut the softwood trees—mostly pine and spruce—and floated the logs down the rivers. Hardwood logs don't float but that didn't always save the hardwood trees. They were cut down wherever they could be dragged to a road, and used for furniture and shipbuilding. Then, when the lumberjacks were through, the farmers moved in. For as long as the residual forest mold lasted, they were able to grow crops.

And I've seen enough in driving around to know this isn't all just past history. The forest is still being used. The loggers can't float logs any more, at least not in New England. Someone decided they were causing ecological damage to the river systems. Now the roads are filled with trucks carrying lumber, water is being diverted from rivers, and thousands of logs are still sluiced daily into the pulp plants along the Penobscot, Kennebec, Androscoggin, and other old logging rivers. Virtually every house along the road has a full season's supply of firewood stacked outside. Lots are advertised for their lumber value, and the Forest Service is forever warning that the forests are not inexhaustible.

Good for you oh wise old Forest Service. I know its other parts of the Federal Government that have done most of the work on controlling acid rain fallout, and I don't believe you're as naïve as some of your literature. However, you do get credit for pushing sensible cautions and, overall, you've done a fine job of forest preservation. And, as you and the locals both know, this is forest land and will continue to be used as such. With or without permission from you or old King George, man will continue to cut the trees and use the wood.

Good for local government and industry too. They are working with the Forest Service to make sure the use is within sound conservation guidelines. Everyone deserves credit because they are doing an intelligent job of working with the geography. And I don't think it is taking anything away from anyone to say I think the geography was going to win anyway.

This is remote northern New England. Trees thrive in this rocky glacial till; crops don't. For about a century now farm acreage has been decreasing; forest cover has been increasing. And the trees came back on their own terms. That's right, they came back to provide shade for Old Archibald's grave. I can't find where any form of European style control was ever considered. Just as well. It wouldn't have worked; too much land, not enough people. Working with nature was the right choice. What we have now is natural growth over tremendously large areas with dead wood lying where it falls, underbrush, wild animals, and, yes, even occasional old goats lurking around the edges in hopes of picking up pretty girls.

These forests are healthy, and a never ending source of discovery and wonder. Even in driving around the edges, there's a lot to see. American Elm trees which, elsewhere, have been wiped out by the Dutch Elm Disease, are tall, strong, and numerous, particularly between Bangor and Skowhegan. The white birches are the standout trees of the forest, especially during this season. Some of the trunks are surprisingly thick, and the off-white color of their bark shows brilliantly against the early autumn colors. They're at their best in the stretch of road just before and after entering New Hampshire. The most romantic discoveries, and I found them without too much mucking around, are the old logs still stuck in the muddy banks of the Penobscot and Connecticut rivers.

There are pleasing wooded vistas almost anywhere you go. The White Mountains are nature on the grand scale and the views are spectacular. The mile after mile of rolling forested hills, broken up by small farm settlements, in Aroostook County, Maine, and the eastern parts of Vermont, are rusticity at its best. And the driving is easy.

People Watching

There are people up here, quite a few of them, who seem to get along fine without being restricted by an occupation. It's an old American idea of independence that seems to be fairly common in parts of New England and the rural South. They work, but that's not the regulating force in their lives. And it's not just home grown natives. Some of the latter day pioneers in the clearings, and people like my waiter friend in Bangor, come from other parts of the country because they can be more relaxed here.

Maybe if the waiter marries his girlfriend, and they have children, things will change. Maybe not. I don't know. A little travel and a few quiet days in the country isn't enough to qualify me as an expert. Besides, I'm just beginning to accept the notion that people can get along without my idea of a regular job. They do odd jobs, grow vegetables, fish, hunt, cut wood, have spare time, and make ends meet. It's a toss up. The job money supplements the natural life, or the natural life supplements the job money. Either way, they seem to know how to live with nature and the rhythms of nature. It's a different talent, a talent I never had. And it doesn't qualify when I throw twigs in a river. I'm always making a game of that. But that's not living with nature, it's playing in it. Nature's a pastime with me, with them it's part of everyday living. I know, too, that they earn their keep, but, and I say this without envy, they seem to have a self assured independence I've never known. Must be something that goes with country living.

No giving up though. There's a place in the country for everyone, including me. There has to be. If nothing else, and despite my usual problems with the bird book, I can ride around and watch and look. Robert Frost, the New Hampshire poet, took some time to watch some woods filling up with snow. That's country too—not the snow but the person taking the time to watch some woods filling up with snow. That's all it takes to be an observer, time—time and patience—time, patience, and a couple of lazy days in the hills of New England.

It's the hills. There's a primitive tug in these remote, rugged, and beautiful hills. Live in the city all your life, see them once, and something says home. They're an invitation to return to the wonders of nature, to live with the mysteries of slow growth. Even as a visitor I get a different sense of time. I consciously started out to take my time. Now I find myself doing it in a more relaxed and natural way. It's the hills, the hills and these people.

Barre, Montpelier, and Admiral George Dewey

Historically, Vermont didn't put up with state government any more than it had to. Montpelier is the capitol. It's spread out longwise along a mountain pass. It's uncluttered and clean. The Greek copy State House, which shows more like a museum than a working building has a fine array of pictures, and a couple of them tell a good history story. We'll get back to that. Otherwise, though, and I'm trying hard to be polite, the best thing that can be said about Montpelier is that it has gotten better, a lot better. It is an interesting and pleasant daytime walking town. But, so far as I am concerned, Barre, which is less than ten miles down the road, is still the place to stay.

There are motels and restaurants, and the eating's good, especially if you like Italian. Originally, it was the Scots who did most of the work in opening up the great granite quarries of Barre. Then the northern Italians moved in and the two groups got along like cousins, especially during prohibition when they were running booze in from nearby Canada. I think all this has something to do with why the town has such nice accommodations, but let's not go into that. The thing to really enjoy here is what they can do with stone.

They ringed a downtown youth memorial with a horseshoe shaped whispering stone bench. I don't know the dimensions. However, if you were sitting at one end of the bench and you wanted to say something to someone who was sitting at the opposite end, you would think you had to shout. But you don't. They worked out the design and acoustics so you can whisper, or talk in a normal voice, and be heard anywhere along the bench. Then, just up the hill from the town square, there's a magnificently casual statue of Robert Burns which some say is the finest statue in America. And, to match this, going down Main Street, there's a newer statue honoring Italian-Americans. These two are as impressive as any statues I've ever seen. And the listing could go on because Barre, which lists itself as the granite capitol of the world, is always happy to show its mining, cutting, carving, and crafting skills. Good tours are available locally and worth the time. But now its time to get back to Montpelier's State House and some Spanish-American War history.

Remember that one? In its own time it was one heck of a war. Everyone was convinced that Spain was mistreating the poor people in a couple of islands they still "owned" in the Caribbean. Exaggerated newspaper accounts made conditions seem worse than they really were. America's duty, as a progressive forward looking nation, was to get involved and straighten out the mess. It all sounds strange now when the thought of war gives more chill than thrill, but then was then and the whole country (in-laws included) seemed to think that war with Spain would be a splendid adventure.

The British poet Kipling, an in-law (his Vermont wife came from a little south of Route 2) wrote a silly poem to let us know that this bully war had something to do with white and duty being the properly matched twin glories of creation. Ignoring this, the blacks joined in, saved the Rough Rider's flanks at the battle of San Juan, and hoped that, somehow or another, things would be better this time. Even the pacifist critics conceded that this was a noble war, one of them went so far as to say it was "the most honorable single war in all history."

So off they went. With a firm belief that their cause was noble and just, with north and south reunited, flags flying, bands playing, and women and children cheering, our boys went off to the most popular and successful war in the history of the United States. Sousa wrote the tunes, and Teddy Roosevelt set the tone.

Looking back I get an impression that this was part of a lifelong standoff between Roosevelt and the American public. He wanted respect—period. The public was determined to give him that along with affection—the kind of affection usually given to children. Part of the Teddy Bear business is the old story of a disgusted Roosevelt refusing to shoot a bear that was tied to a tree. But it's more than just that. He did look the part, and the public was really taken up with the Teddy Bear fad. Roosevelt accepted it. He couldn't find any way to avoid it. But he didn't understand about the goofy stuffed bears, and he much preferred being called Theodore.

So, like it or not, the caricature became part of his public life. Teddy was a stocky fellow with a bushy mustache, big front teeth, and a strong jaw. He was a cartoonist's delight. His ambitions, programs, energy levels, and animal magnetism infected a whole generation of Americans. One of his political followers quipped, "Roosevelt bit me and I went mad." And a good part of this mystique and caricature dates back to Teddy's Spanish American War record, especially his charge up San Juan hill. It was a heroic action by a man who went on to Presidential greatness. It is the sort of thing that leaves a lasting impression. It is still the picture that comes most readily to mind when mention is made of the Spanish American War. However, without taking anything away from Teddy, he was not the number one hero of the Spanish American War. That honor belongs to Montpelier's Admiral George Dewey.

Montpelier's State House has two prominent pictures of Admiral Dewey. The one in the main lobby is an action picture of the battle. We'll get back to that. In the upstairs portrait he looks stern and healthy. His own age thought he was handsome, but, like so many other things, I guess that's a matter of taste. He's a little too old, and formal to be handsome by modern standards, but he still looks like a hero. He's in full dress uniform, and wearing the jeweled sword that Congress ordered from Tiffany's. And, even now, there's something reassuring about the military bearing, full gray mustache, solid features, and direct gaze. This is a man comfortable with command. He was the idol of my grandparent's generation, and the one who showed the world that America had come of age. He was the hero of the battle of Manila Bay.

The verdict was in doubt on that clear day in April, 1898 when Admiral Dewey led our Pacific Squadron out of Hong Kong. His destination was Manila, the capitol city of the Spanish held Philippine Islands. He had studied available intelligence reports, he had his plan of attack, and he intended to win. But there wasn't any solid information on the Spanish state of readiness and, certainly, there was no guarantee of victory. In fact, British sailors in Hong Kong expected that we would lose. Their sympathy was with us, though, and the sailors of a nearby British ship crowded the deck to give a final cheer to our brave men who were sailing off to death.

Picking up on the insights and feelings of another age is difficult. In this case it is especially difficult. We know the Spaniards were almost completely unprepared. And, since then, we have seen so many large and horrible battles. With all this, the Battle of Manila Bay becomes an encounter, in an almost forgotten war, in which we outgunned a Spanish squadron. Dewey becomes yesterday's hero, and not a hero for the ages. That's the verdict of history and it is undoubtedly correct. But historic verdicts are hindsight.

Forget hindsight. Remember courage and glory. Our crews braved the threat of coastal guns, mines, torpedoes, and return salvos when they steamed into Manila Bay, none of which happened. But our men had no way of knowing none of this would happen. They went in and fought. Then, after destroying the Spanish squadron, Dewey isolated the shore garrison by cutting the communication cable. It was a good tactical move. However, because of this, no word could get out of Manila. America couldn't find out what happened. It became the home front's time to have second thoughts about the risks of war.

The press had made the war moral and right. Teddy made it a test of courage. Sousa's band toured the country, and the war effort became a heart thumping, throat lumping, patriotic thrill. Public support was strong, emotional, and positive. But fear's target is confidence, and now it had its own good shot at the public mood. Our Pacific squadron had steamed into far off Manila Bay and disappeared. It was swallowed up, gone without a trace. People remembered other things. President McKinley had warned about our lack of preparation. The British saw things that way too. They thought Spain would win because, on paper, their navy was better than ours. What happened to our Pacific squadron? Why weren't the Spaniards sending anything out over their cable?

For three weeks America and the world had to wait and wonder. The rumor was disaster, and the public braced itself for the bad news. Word finally came. It was victory, total victory. It was the end of Spain as a Pacific power. Our men were alive and well, and we were the Pacific power of the new age. America went into a state of wild celebration. Admiral Dewey became the hero of the age.

As time went on, and the public got to know him better, he became even more of a popular idol. It was as if some noble person had come to life from one of Kipling's better poems. The man really was a fine example of so much that was good in our civilization, and he suited the tastes of the age. With a decent private income, he was the self assured gentleman of public affairs, and very much at ease in the clubs and meeting rooms of the nation's capitol. Also, as a commander, he was admired by his peers, and respected by his men. He was the beau ideal of his age and, for an added touch of romance, he was a handsome widower.

Those were the good old days, the days when gray haired men were regarded as handsome and romantic, bravery was honored, virtue was praised, and success was admired. Vermont doesn't forget. Our grandparents would be pleased to know the action picture is still in the main lobby. It's a battle scene done in the grand manner. Dewey's in Manila Bay, standing on a deck that's elevated above one of the gun turrets, and gazing into the smoke of battle. Gaze on Admiral. Like Keats's fair youth, your image is frozen in your own time and, there, you'll always be a handsome hero.

<u>Farms</u>

Jim Hill, a railroad man and western promoter back in the 1800s, used to tell crowds that New Englanders planted crops by filling a shotgun with seed and shooting it up a hill. It got laughs out west. So far as I know, he never came to New England to tell that story, but it doesn't matter. He probably would have got laughs here too. New England born Henry Adams went even further, he carried on about Yankees trying to grow crops from granite. No one objected. Most everyone here accepts any bad or funny thing said about New England farming.

Agri is the culture that gives New Englanders an inferiority complex. Somewhere along the line the rocky subsoil and glacial till became an acceptable excuse for failed farmers and gardeners. Not growing things almost becomes a way of life. It is a mind-set that grows and travels with you—well, all right then, with me. Even down in Maryland's soft coastal plain I gaze in wonder at how everyone else can have such nice lawns and gardens while I'm still having trouble getting zoysia to take in my back yard. Deep down I know it's not the soil or the plugs, it's me. It is a predisposition for failure I brought down from New England. I think I can't and so on.

This isn't a put on. It's real, and it's not just me. For many of us it was a basic part of growing up in the town and city parts of New England. James Russell Lowell went without because he couldn't bring himself to press a delinquent farm tenant for rent. The otherwise brilliant Mr. Lowell thought it would be wrong to pester someone who actually could and did grow crops. What the farmer was doing was some kind of wonder of wonders. It's a New England attitude. But it wouldn't make sense in any other part of America and it shouldn't make sense here either. This is one New England attitude that is just plain wrong.

So when I get back to Maryland I'll work on my attitude and my back yard. For now, though, I'm trying to figure out how Adams, Lowell, and so many other native detractors could have been so wrong. My guess is they were reflecting on the history of their times, local failures, and western gains.

Part of it would go back to the farmers who had to give up on the forest land. New England folklore is filled with stories of harsh conditions that resulted from whole generations trying to grow crops on unproductive land. The ruins are still in evidence, and the best crop turned out to be the hard working people who came from these poor families. And, during these same times, the Midwest and Western areas were taking over the wheat and cattle business. Those were discouraging times, but they were not the end of northern New England's business, at least not on the good land. A little research, and sunny day driving around, shows that local farmers went on, quietly and successfully, with the business of growing crops.

The farms are small. There's a limited labor supply, the land is hilly, and, even on the good land, there's glacial debris. As the land was cleared, the stones were set aside for later use; it took generations of family labor to build those stone walls. The barns are huddled close to the houses, frequently with enclosed connecting walkways, and this provides a picturesque arrangement. The purpose, of course, is to protect farmer and livestock during long cold winters.

Transportation and competition have always been problems. Aroostook County has good farmland and fair rainfall, but farming wasn't profitable until the railroad was built. Even then, it was necessary to specialize in potatoes because they didn't have to arrive fresh. Pork was a staple on colonial farms, and salted pork was sold in the old sailing days. Beef was commercially successful in both the Champlain and Connecticut River valleys. Wheat was grown in several areas and, until after the Civil War, there was a flourishing sheep business. The Midwestern farm areas took over most of these markets as the railroads pushed west. New England farmers had to adjust.

New England industry had to adjust too. The shoe and leather business had been built on cattle hides. Boston's preeminence in the wool business was based on sheep from these northern farms. Even the venerable distillery business had to give ground.

This distillery business, incidentally, had nothing to do with the New England rum that historians always talk about. That had a bad name. Artemus Ward ridiculed its taste. The Indians preferred French brandy. Even the settlers sought alternatives, barley and apple trees were among the first crops planted. But the historic rum was a Massachusetts product. The distillery business in these northern areas was whiskey and beer, and, back in the 1800s, it was a booming industry that provided good cash revenues for New England farmers.

Those were the developing years. Mills and factories were being built. Railroads and canals were opening the interior. Labor gangs, construction crews, and itinerant workers were everywhere. It was a time of cheap liquor, heavy drinking, temperance movements, and prohibition laws that didn't work. Maine, for example, had an early prohibition law, but the rule in Bangor was that grog merchants would pay an annual fine and be otherwise left alone. But this is straying from the farm discussion. Back to the subject.

Business was lost to the western areas and adjustments were made. Today's farming is an assortment of what works. Potato farming still dominates the Aroostook County economy. It's hard work and the market fluctuates. But it's a crop with a steady demand. It's a staple and, as they love to point out, potatoes are low in calories. The old Indian crops—corn, beans, squash, and pumpkins—are still popular. Trees, especially maple and apple, do well in this soil. More favorably located farms have concentrated on commodities that can be delivered fresh to New England's industrial cities—dairy products, eggs, and vegetables. Overall, the average cash value per acre is high, and the farms are holding their place in a competitive market.

Farming doesn't dominate the land, but it's here and it's an important part of the economy. The farms are tucked into a forested landscape. You drive over a hill, around a turn, or into a clearing, and there's a farm. It belongs. With over two hundred years of development and adjustment, the farms blend in with their surroundings. They fit in the mountain valleys and the occasional level land on the sides of hills. They fit in the narrow Connecticut River and Champlain valleys with a natural waterway in the center and the hills for a backdrop. They've earned their part of the landscape. It's only a part, but New England wouldn't be New England without its farms and farm families.

Burlington

As usual, Burlington took me by surprise. The driving has been slow and relaxed since Bangor, and I just wasn't prepared for Vermont's one real city. I get to the point, especially on some of the more rural stretches of Route 2, where I begin to believe its normal to poke along, stop wherever I want just to take a picture or look at a barn, and then pull out on the road again. It's undisciplined driving. I paralleled Interstate Route 89 in a few places and I could see the disciplined traffic speeding along. I wasn't part of it and I was smug enough to feel superior to it. Most of the time I was the only car on my old road. I stayed with the natural valley route, weaving in and out with the Winooski River and following around the contours of hills until, all of a sudden, I was in city traffic. Ready or not, I was in Burlington. I had arrived at the end of New England.

Yankee dominance ends on the shores of Lake Champlain. New England settlers worked up from both south and east, arrived here in full vigor, and found that other settlers had claim to all the adjacent lands. New York starts on the western side of the lake; Quebec is to the north. Maybe that's why Burlington is so boldly New England. It's the last place where the culture could be dominant.

It's just the dominance that stopped here, by the way, not the culture, and certainly not the people. They went on to become part of the mix all across America. Canals were completed from the southern part of this lake to the Hudson River, and across New York State to the Great Lakes. New Englanders poured through Burlington and other cities, followed the waterways, and settled all across the land. The restless, failed farmers, missionaries, traders, lumber jacks, teachers, the extra children of large families—they moved on and influenced the national culture. But, for all their drive and influence, they couldn't really recreate New England in other parts of this country. The Yankee domain ended on the shores of Lake Champlain. Burlington is its final city.

Originally, of course, no thought was given to building any place as an end to a culture. This was just another place to settle and do business. Still, it must have been thrilling to discover a location with so much beauty and so many natural advantages. There was a navigable lake which connected to British Canada and New York State, a good bay, timber, rich valley farmland, and a river that reached back to the center of Vermont. It started, naturally enough, as a shipping center for Vermont's lumber and farm products. With this location it had to happen. There had to be a medium size city here. Fortunately, with New England charm, a city was built to compliment the location. Fortunately, too, it is easy to wander around and understand the place. Trees aren't the only things that show well in this state. History and the forces of nature are more noticeable here, or at least it seems that way to some of us.

Thomas Jefferson, for one, probably came to believe that nature and history were one and the same thing in this part of the country. He never got to see Burlington. The wind was against him on his early northern tour and he couldn't get across from the New York side of Lake Champlain. He didn't like the lake anyway, he said it was "turbulent." Later, when he was President, he tried to stop shipping from United States ports. The wind was still against him.

His Embargo Acts almost worked. Great Britain did give up some of their more obnoxious policies just at the time we were declaring war. Historians, however, still argue as to whether or not the embargo was a practical idea. Arguments aside, New England resisted it, and Burlington was a center of resistance. Jefferson, and Madison after him, found out that these people could be every bit as turbulent as the waters of Lake Champlain. The locals did business with British Canada during both the Embargo and the War of 1812. And they defended their right to do this business. Guns were carried on rafts and, in the event of capture and arrest by Federal officials, local juries consistently refused to come in with guilty findings. The city gained a dubious reputation. Some years later Nathaniel Hawthorne, a staunch Democrat, sarcastically described Burlington as a place where, "British and American coins are jumbled in the same pockets, the effigies of the King of England being made to kiss those of the Goddess of Liberty."

An interesting sidelight is knowing that there was an election while all this was going on. Jefferson was stepping down. His friend Madison was running for the Presidency. New England, except for Vermont, voted against Madison. I can't explain the politics. I don't know why the people of Vermont voted for Madison, but they did. Score one for Madison. Score one for the state too. In the most stand alone part of America, Vermont stands by itself.

In reviewing this old history, it helps to remember that these were a people whose ancestors crossed the ocean because they insisted on their right to stand alone. Dissent and resistance to authority were part of their heritage. They were Puritans, and here, I think it might help if we clarify some terms. Puritan includes Pilgrim and Congregationalist. As a religion, they're all the same. The name comes from old England where these people tried to "purify" the beliefs and practices of the Anglican Church. One group of them left for Holland where they could practice their own Puritan beliefs. They were off on this trip for religious reasons; it was a pilgrimage. They were the Pilgrims and they were the group that went on to settle Plymouth, Massachusetts. They were joined by the main body of believers from England who set up in Boston, Massachusetts. They were all Puritans. Then, to avoid domination by the Church of England, they decentralized and said each church congregation could have responsibility

For its own church management, hence, they were Congregationalists.

And all this, by the way, explains some of why Yankee culture didn't take over anywhere else. Its church was disorganized. Other churches fared better. The Presbyterians, to take one example, had the same basic beliefs as the Puritans, but Presbyterianism was the official religion of Scotland. These believers weren't avoiding any mother church. They had a lower dissent level. They were able to exercise more centralized control, and, in the long run, this gave them better organization, discipline, and lasting power.

On the other hand, though, the Puritans were the great educators of early America, and they turned out to be a surprisingly progressive group. I think it was in part because of the independence of their churches, maybe another part had to do with their quest for God's truth. Even old Cotton Mather, a New England minister who the historian J.C. Furnas referred to as an "ordained calamity" because his writings contributed to the witch hunt, gets some credit for being a progressive. Mather and others did work hard at trying to uncover the truth. All those sincere and honest efforts to figure out God's plans so they could work along with them did lead to improved knowledge and some unexpected fallout. Businesses benefited, which was just fine. Puritans never had anything against prosperity. History books became more reliable. Nature and medical studies became more scientific. Old

Cotton was involved in much of this, and he was especially involved in the fight to have people accept inoculation. And all this, of course, is leading us away from their religion.

The Presbyterian kirk is still here and doing fine. The old Puritan based colleges are spread across America. Most of the old Congregational churches, however, have been absorbed by reorganization into other church groups. There are still some stand alone Congregational churches holding out and practicing whatever it is their congregations decide to practice. Whatever it is, though, it isn't the old Puritanism. In both colleges and churches, that's dead. Who said so? Not me. I wouldn't take it on myself to make that kind of pronouncement. No, it wasn't me, it was several other people, the poet, Dr. Oliver Wendell Holmes, and Harriet Beecher Stowe, the author of Uncle Tom's Cabin, to name just two.

Stowe's husband, father, and brother were ordained ministers, originally Puritan in their beliefs but, as time went on, she and her husband, although they stayed religious, just dropped the Puritan parts of their beliefs. And they were among the last to do so. Even in their day, it was fast becoming a thing of the past. Holmes agreed. His poem of the "One Hoss Shay" was about the breakup of the old Puritan beliefs. And his father, too, was a Puritan minister.

But these people were as pleasant and polite as could be as they left the old faith. All that predestination preaching of God's plans and who was and wasn't among the "elect" seemed harsh to outsiders. And it undoubtedly was, at least at times. All I can offer by way of explanation is Rosemary and Stephen Vincent Benet's observation on the Adams family, their faults were their own, "but their virtues were the nation's." This and the feelings of people who more or less knew them, Mrs. Stowe, Dr. Holmes, and me. As she broke off from the faith, she went out of her way to show the old Puritans as an amiable people. His poem showed that the church was a wonderfully built thing. And, on a personal basis, I must say that when I did some earlier work on different places around the country that were settled by New Englanders, I wound up fond of the Puritans. I only met them in old books and diaries, but I found out about how they prayed, drank, preached, joked, and set up schools wherever they could. All in all I found very little of the arrogance you would expect from people who believed themselves to be the "elect." I found them to be a friendly and decent group, and the trait that impressed me most was their attitude toward family. They loved family, perhaps more so than any other group that ever lived in America. Family was their main indulgence.

Their houses still show well in Burlington. They're the lovingly built spacious Victorian homes that rim the downtown area. As pointed out earlier, I've lost some notes, but my recollection is that these were singled out once as the greatest remaining set of Victorian homes in America. Whatever, they're a living tribute to family life. And you can sense that the original owners had to be self confident and satisfied with life when they built these sturdy houses with overlooking views of the city and lake. Their churches are still here too. For pure New England and simple sacredness, there's nothing that can compare with old Congregational churches. In this part of New England, they're the ones with the columns in front, and squat bell towers on the roof. They're clean solid buildings with dignity, reserve, and grace—appropriate places for worship. And, considering they were Puritans, the valley setting must have reinforced their beliefs in God's plans.

From the beach at Leddy Park, on the north side of Burlington, you can look across the water to the end of a peninsula called Rock Point (binoculars help) and see different colored rock layers. The interest lies in knowing that, because of ancient compressive forces from the east, there was crustal earth movement. The top red layer is older than the lower black layer. This is a visible section of the Champlain over thrust that extends through to Canada. From a tourist's point of view, this is just a fun thing to see. But it is also part of the overall geology that, large or small, is so telling here.

The Green Mountains are on the Vermont side, the Adirondack Mountains are on the New York side, and Lake Champlain is in the valley between. It's still big and beautiful, but not as big as it used to be. It's a receding remnant of a glacial lake that once occupied the whole valley. It worked down to its present level in stages. The series of fertile terraces between the lake and the Green Mountains are from various high water stages. And it shows well in Burlington, especially in the area south of downtown. The city climbs up, level by level from the lake. This is why each street full of houses has its own grand view. But the point here is that the terraces, along with the valley climate, is the basis for the farm wealth. This is the narrowest of a connected series of valleys that run from the St. Lawrence lowland to Alabama. Some southern air works its way up these valleys and gives just enough climate modification to provide an increased growing season. It's a great setup but what, if anything, does it mean?

Cotton Mather said God kept a veil over New England until the "elect" were ready to cross the ocean. Puritans could see God's design in just about everything, and this valley must have seemed the ultimate in God's long range plan for his chosen people. But their own university led them, or their children, away from these beliefs. They built the University of Vermont within easy walking distance of downtown Burlington. It's a nice place, we'll get back to it later. Right now I'm more concerned with one of its famous graduates, John Dewey, an important American progressive philosopher. Back in the 1870s, when he went here, the school was still little more than a Puritan training ground. The lessons took, at least for a while. Dewey was a religious believer when he left here but, as the years went on, he changed his thinking. He abandoned his religious beliefs. Personally, though, I think he held on to some early valley lessons, and it shows in his mature philosophy.

Simple examples can be overstated and, with Dewey, I'm dealing with a complex and sophisticated personality. He went on from here to major university assignments in Minnesota, Chicago, and New York, and universal fame as an educational innovator and a philosopher. His writings have become part of the world's literature. Still, I'm convinced that part of his genius was a throwback to Puritan conditioning and still another part was a reflection of plain old Champlain Valley geography.

Dewey used arguments that were based on the totality of experience. Understanding of people should be based on their history, the geography that influenced the history, weather, the geologic and climatic conditions that created the geography and weather and so on. He lost his early Puritan belief in predestination, God's design for the world and its inhabitants. Then he philosophized about the shaping forces of nature and history. The theology parts of his school lessons were discarded. Natural design took over and I think this powerful valley homeland of his became a part of the new progressive beliefs.

Dewey prevailed, at least in the social end of things. Those of us who are old enough can remember seeing his pictures in newspapers into the 1950s. He seemed like a gentle old man, still active in philosophy, and still an activist in education and social movements. The world had changed since his youth, and he was one of the architects of change, especially in the field of education. The changes were fundamental as well as necessary, and there's no reconciling Dewey with the Puritans. Still, we can't totally discard the historic base that was, in fact, Puritan. Even in Dewey's terms, the old timers couldn't be all wrong. They lived with the valley. They were the history. They built the city, and it was their school.

Walt Whitman again: "Wisdom is not finally tested in schools. Wisdom cannot be pass'd from one having it to another not having it." True Walt, true. And we still don't know how to test wisdom. But you'd be pleased to know we've made progress in democratizing the schools. Sex, race, and lack of money aren't the barriers they used to be. And the University of Vermont, which has one of the most beautiful campuses in America, has a good record in this area. They can't promise wisdom, but they're doing what they can to promote education. And, by the way, although they seem to be even stronger in science, their curriculum is still strong in the humanities, areas such as religion, philosophy, and English, including some interesting looking poetry courses. Like so many things up here, the university still reflects credit on its origins.

It's obvious that the earlier settlers treated this location with respect, and took delight and pride in their charming little city. They had their school and churches in the neighborhood, and their homes overlooked the business houses and the bay. This came close to being the earthly fulfillment of their beliefs. This was the world as God intended it to be. Maybe the creed did predestine their success. Then again, the old beliefs have faded and the city's still a prosperous and pleasant place. Dewey's undoubtedly right, it's a matter of geography and history. The history, however, is Puritan—and my thinking is getting circular. Whatever the background and beliefs, it's still a great little city.

The new continues to build on the old and, without any loss of attractiveness, Burlington is a modern city. The electronic industries, which are located in the suburbs, have attracted new people. Lake shipping is pretty much a thing of the past, but downtown is still a commercial center. There's a good variety of hotels, motels, restaurants, and shopping places. The thing that surprises me most, though, is my own reaction. I'm enjoying the simple thrill of being back in a city.

Life is exciting. Traffic is complicated and fast. People on the sidewalks are alert and moving with a purpose. It's a challenge. I want to move with the rhythms of this commercial hubbub. It's all right to relax and poke around on the lakefront, the Victorian neighborhoods, and the campus, but en route, I act like a man with a purpose. It becomes important to show that I'm not fuddy duddy, to show myself, in fact, that I can keep up with the pace. I even found myself being more conscious of grooming. After all, what's the fun of going out in a city if you can't dress up and look as neat as the other people.

It probably has something to do with the charm of the city. It's still a place with a lot of the old delight and pride. The people live in the present but they know how to preserve the past, and they're good at promoting the enjoyment of this beautiful natural setting. Even the ambitious downtown shopping mall, with it's "Lakeview" garage overlook of the waterfront area, is a pleasant, nicely renovated blend of old and new. Battery Park, though, is the best place for views. From there you can see the bay, the waterfront, the expanse of the lake, and the mountains. And, with all the modern improvements, there's still a lot that hasn't changed. The old houses still reign, well kept and majestic, on their tree lined streets. Business continues downtown. The churches are still active places of worship, and geography still dominates the valley.

Rouses Point

It's about thirty miles from Burlington to the end of this segment of Route 2. The road swings around to the north of the city, through some rough hill country, and then crosses a bridge to an island in the center of Lake Champlain. From there to the end its all island and peninsula, pleasant rolling country with views of the lake from one, the other, and sometimes both sides of the road.

The road crosses a bridge to Rouses Point, New York and a sign says "End Route 2." That's it. There's a north-south road, an arrow pointing north to Canada, and a border station. This is where the eastern segment of Route 2 ends. Those 1926 map makers studied the situation, ended it here, and picked it up again in Sault Ste. Marie, Michigan. It was a logical decision.

The United States can't have an east-west highway at this latitude because of the Great Lakes, and a big southern dip of Ontario, Canada. That's one of the reasons I'm on this road. I wanted the trip to include Canada. But just about any northern routing could have given me this. With the way this border was drawn, neither country can have a direct east-west highway flow, not at this latitude.

There are still Canadian writers who criticize the old British negotiators for this. They think that, if knowledgeable Canadians were included in the treaty negotiations, Canada might have come out with a more advantageous geographic position. The Americans, so the argument goes, had the advantage over the British because of their better understanding of North American geography, and the importance of various water routes. Personally, I think both sides did a pretty good partisan job of seeking advantage. Whatever else, it made for an interesting border.

Just run your finger along the lines of a good map and see what you find. The eastern half of our boundary is a combination of artificial lines and meandering waterways. It's part history, part geography, part mistake, part absurdity, and all compromise. Both countries came out of the negotiations with routing problems. The trans Canada Highway has to swing more than a hundred miles to the north to avoid the State of Maine. And this cross Canada course I'm following is, in fact, the only direct land route from here to the upper Midwestern areas of the United States.

The two countries intersect and overlap, and, just following the border as it weaves along the water courses, anyone can see that every square foot was negotiated. This island for me, that island for you, this large island for me, those two small islands for you, and so it goes for more than a thousand miles along the St. Lawrence River and the Great Lakes. It even got to the point where we have two isolated peninsulas surrounded by the Canadian land mass, one in Lake of the Woods, Minnesota, and the other on the west coast just south of Vancouver. The west coast one is understandable; it's on our side of the 49th degree line. The Minnesota peninsula was just a misunderstanding of Midwestern geography, but it's where the line was drawn and it's ours. Then again, there's that Madawaska leg in the Province of New

Brunswick that, at one time, was claimed by Maine. Neither country has ever willingly given up a square foot of land.

Since the stand off we had in the War of 1812, however, both sides have learned to compromise. War doesn't help. Even where mistakes have been made, things can be worked out. This part of the border, for example, is just a little north of the agreed upon 45th degree of north latitude. What happened is that an earlier survey had been in error, and the United States built a fort, here in Rouses Point, to command the Richelieu River entrance to Lake Champlain. When a new survey was taken we discovered that our fort was above the 45th line.

It was an honest mistake and, understandably, we didn't want to give up a fort that was both expensive and strategic. This was, after all, the invasion route in both of our wars with Great Britain. The problem was resolved peacefully, and we kept our fort. The old erroneous survey line, the "false 45th" as it is sometimes called, was accepted as part of a package that included those irregular borders of New Hampshire and Maine. And here the boundary still sits, just above the 45th line. But our once mighty fort is nothing but a picturesque ruin which, sorry to say, is not open to the public.

However, Fort Montgomery, as it is called, can be seen from the bridge that leads to Rouses Point. There is a pull off landing where people can park their cars, get out, and gaze across the water at the fort. You can't miss it. It's the only thing there, and it looks good from a distance. It looks like it is still guarding the entrance to Lake Champlain. Fact is, though, that it is no longer up to the job. The fort that changed the boundary is now an unmarked ruin on the world's longest unprotected border.

MONTREAL—QUEBEC

Francis Parkman and History

It would be interesting sometime to trace the historic similarities and differences between Montreal and Boston. They were match and offset for each other all the way from here to the Pacific. They started, shaped, and developed so much of what we have today in North America. It was Puritan missionaries from one, Jesuits, Franciscans, and nuns from the other. Each took a turn at developing sites along the Great Lakes, places that have since become great cities. Montreal went on west by land, Boston by sea and they met on the Pacific slope to compete for the fur and carrying trade of the old Oregon Territory. Both grew rich. Both built prestige schools and set standards for quality education. And both poured their money back into western railroads. But, so far as I know, no one has written a history along these lines.

Fortunately, though, there is good coverage of the early part of the story. Francis Parkman wrote a series of books describing the struggles of the English, French, and Indians for control of North America. He put his all into it. As a young fellow he started his career by heading out west so he could find out what it was like to be an Indian. And he spent a lot of his time covering up the fact that he was frequently sick.

I can't believe he fooled the Sioux, though, not on a simple matter like this. It was not their way to put up with sick people from other places, and they would have noticed Parkman being sick. They were an observant people, and Indian camps were close quarters. They knew. They had to have known, but they let him live anyway.

It must have been for their own reasons. It wasn't for fear of the U.S. Army. It was the year 1846 and the nearest army post was more than six hundred miles to the east. These Sioux had no fear of the army.

Love didn't have anything to do with it either. Parkman wasn't lovable. He came with a hired guide, and there was a thin pretext of belonging. Basically, though, he was a self invited guest in an Indian camp. And this unusual guest always slept with a stick beside him. He would use it to hit Indian children "miniature savages" as he called them, over the head whenever they tried to share his body warmth or blanket.

Maybe the Sioux thought he had more Indian type virtues than anyone else they ever met. This young white stoic never spared himself. He never gave in to his sickness. He never shirked or avoided any of the hardships having to do with riding, hunting, or camping. And he was obviously a driven young fellow. He was bound and determined to know what it felt like to be an Indian. Maybe that was it. Maybe the Indians recognized the intensity of his drive and thought he was possessed by spirits. Maybe he was.

Near as I can figure it, Francis Parkman never spared himself—or anyone else. He was one of those people who could be accurate without being sympathetic, honest without being merciful, and good without being kind. His simple decency, however, kept him from going sour, and his understanding was such that every so often he would even make allowance for feelings. Most of all, though, Francis was a brilliant defender of the values of civilization and rationality. And, so far as he was concerned, the Anglo-Saxon race was the keeper of the values.

This was an understandable belief, at least in his case. He was a proper Bostonian of the 1800s and, it follows, a Harvard graduate. Only someone with this background could make a point of recognizing that the lower classes have feelings. Here he is on the early Dutch settlers of Schenectady, New York: "They were simple peasants and woodsmen, but with human affections and capable of human woe."

It's typical Parkman, direct and blunt with no hesitation about putting people in their place. Even the English, especially those who were original settlers in Virginia, came in for periodic drubbings. But, overall, the English make out well. They're more masculine and more capable of self government. The French are generally venal and given over to incessant supernaturalism. Montreal, for example, was believed by pious French people to have been founded in response to miraculous visions from Heaven. Parkman refers to one of the founders as, "This miserable victim of illusions." Next come the Indians. They're squalid superstitious savages who didn't have the ability or intelligence to create a civilization. In this he cited some of those nineteenth century cranium and brain size studies that were thought to be scientific. Regardless of the reasons, Francis Parkman wasn't gentle with other peoples races and religions.

Yet, there's a difference. Francis wasn't a bigot. He studied. He kept his mind open. He took that trip out west, lived with the Indians, and he did all he could to understand them. And when all was said and done, in his own gruff and honest way, he respected them. They wasted their advantages, fought each other, burned settlements, tortured prisoners, and resisted civilization. Francis was too much a believer in civilization to condone their actions. Still, he did understand. He described their simple equality and independence, their codes of honor, their deliberations, pride, passions, celebrations and hunts, the changes wrought by civilization, the glories of victory, and the suffering of defeat. Despite his bluntness and bias, Francis Parkman was a sensitive recorder of the Indian's losing struggle to retain a tribal way of life.

Most of all, though, Francis discovered the romance of old French Canada. It was a different world. It wasn't like the old New England he knew so well. The French had settlements but they didn't come to occupy the country. They came to convert the Indians, to trade, and to explore. And Francis captured all of it. He was the one outside historian with the depth, understanding, and energy to do full justice to this greatest of all challenges to English speaking North America. With near total disregard for his failing health, he went on year after year researching, writing, and dictating page after page of vigorous explanation and vivid description. And it all comes back to life.

This was a land of bush rangers, the tough Canadian woodsmen who roamed the forests, and lived and fought on equal terms with the savages. This was a country of aristocrats, court politicians, soldiers, habitants, mystics, profiteers, martyrs, coquettes, and adventurers. This was an extravagant world, a world of piety, privilege, gambling, dancing, gayety, corruption, miracles, and Lenten fasts. This was the world that captivated Francis Parkman.

Montreal was the frontier town of this old Canada. It was the home of the bush rangers. It was the starting point for the explorations of the Great Lakes, the Ohio, the Mississippi, and the great plains through to the Rocky Mountains. It was host to hundreds of painted and feathered Indians who came in fur laden canoes for the annual fair. It was the military center for the wars against both the Iroquois and the English.

I expect there are vestiges somewhere of this old Montreal. I didn't find them. The guide books talk of part of an old seminary wall, and they say Des Commissaires Street is winding because it replaced an old fortified wall. These things ask too much from the imagination. This time I tried the old town, down where the streets are still cobblestone, Rue de la Commune, Place Jaques Cartier, and along the waterfront. It's all very pleasant although it's hard to imagine a primitive shore and brave little sailing ships bobbing up and down on the great river. Then, too, I became distracted by the old buildings and statues, And, so long as I'm at it, the river channels also deserve some attention. The one on the Montreal side is the Lachine canal, an early water route to the Ottawa River. The modern route to the Great Lakes, the St. Lawrence Seaway, is on the opposite shore, the other side of a few thin islands. Wonderful stuff, but I set the time aside to search for the distant past and I'm not doing very well.

There's a statue of Sieur de Maisonneuve, one of the founders, pious, but a good active fellow. He's not the one Parkman called a "miserable victim." There are pictures. The old history is shown on stain glass windows in Notre Dame, and the paintings at the Mount Royal Chalet. It lives on in pictures, statues, and the memory of the people. It isn't lost. This couldn't happen. After all, this is Montreal, the final French bastion. This is where the French army was forced to surrender and, so far as Parkman was concerned, the French King, Louis XV, should never be forgiven for the sad ending and the loss of his North American subjects.

Anyone who has read Parkman knows that his hero was the French General, the Marquis of Montcalm. There's praise and wonder for the enduring gallantry of the general and his troops. The "butterflies of Versailles" showed they could fight "as gaily as they danced." But their skill and bravery was wasted. The King squandered his resources on a foolish European war: he abandoned the tough habitants and loyal troops in Canada. The end was inevitable.

Montcalm was dead. Quebec City and the forts along Lake Ontario and Lake Champlain had fallen. Three British armies with seventeen thousand men had surrounded Montreal. The battered French army had just over two thousand men, yet they offered to fight one more battle. It couldn't be. The civilian governor accepted the surrender terms. French Canada ceased to have a separate existence. And Francis Parkman of Boston became the chief mourner.

Notre Dame

There's a philosophic, maybe even a religious difference, between the inside and the outside of Notre Dame, Montreal's great parish church. The outside, the building itself, has the solid comfortable look of an institution at peace with itself and the world. It's a reflection of French Canada of the 1820s.

Montcalm, French kings, and empire were things of the past. Time had brought changes. Anti-religious revolutionaries had captured France. French Canadians, who were still a religious people, raised voluntary subscriptions to help the British in a war against the old homeland. France would never again be home, and there really wasn't any place else to consider. The United States couldn't fit the bill. French Canadians fought against us in the War of 1812. On reflection, one had to admit that the British had been generally fair rulers. It was a time of peace and good feeling. There was freedom of religion and the protection of British law. Canada was home and, all things considered, a pretty good one. On with the business of life.

In Montreal, incidentally, the business of life usually seems to come around to quality. Quality, class, call it what you will, it's impressive. That's not a first impression of course. The first things noticed up here are size, crowding, and confused traffic patterns. It's in walking around that you notice the nice things. There are surprising discoveries that make city touring a real pleasure, alleys crowded with painting displays, outdoor cafes, flower carts, a variety of restaurants, and even a classical garden at rooftop level. I don't know whether it's French genius, competition between the races, both, or neither. Whatever, I'm straying from my concern with the 1820s.

The parish of Notre Dame decided to build the greatest church in North America. James O'Donnell, a Protestant Irishman practicing in New York City, won the competitive award. His design was English gothic in style, the height of fashion at the time. The church wardens judged it to be the best design and they were satisfied with O'Donnell's credentials. Religion and race didn't matter. He was the man for the job and the contract was signed.

Looking back it seems like a relaxed time, a time when people, at least these people could work with understanding and trust. Ground and elevation problems were resolved. Engineering details were worked out for support of the colossal roof. O'Donnell conscientiously watched costs. The work was community based and part of the labor was from unpaid volunteers. The durable blue-gray limestone came from a local quarry. Bricklayers were trained. It was necessary to have just the right amount of mortar between bricks. The wardens approved all details and approved O'Donnell's performance.

The main structure was opened to the public in 1829. The interior was plain but functional. There weren't any statues for the three large niches above the portico, they'd be provided later. The towers came later too; they weren't finished in O'Donnell's lifetime. These things had to wait. The parish, the wardens, and O'Donnell were exhausted. They had put in five years of dedication and they could do no more. Funds had run out. O'Donnell, who had converted to the Catholic faith, was dying. He lived until after the dedication, and he was buried under the church. The great work of the 1820s was finished.

Now the church is in the middle of a skyscraper area. It still looks solid and sound; the bricklayers did their job well. There's a good view of the front, but restricted side views. Otherwise, though, the setting doesn't matter. Notre Dame has the dignity and grace to fit any setting. It tells the story of serenity and faith, acceptance of this world and belief in the hereafter.

The interior tells a different story. It's a story that, I'm sorry to say, I find discomforting. But that probably tells more about me than the church. Each of us has our own way of looking at things, our own notions and limitations. Then, too, part of my problem is with the

Robert Mac Kinnon

politics of the situation. The interior dates back to an age of friction, and a conservative movement for which I have little sympathy.

The interior, as we see it now, dates primarily from the 1870s, the time of the Quebec "Holy War." Catholic conservatives were attacking liberalism and modernism. Liberals were fighting for change. It was a bitter struggle that lasted throughout the lifetime of most of the participants. It was a time without compromise or surrender. Every issue was tested and fought. Bishops and politicians were found hard and fast on both sides. In some dioceses it was a sin to vote for Wilfred Laurier, or any candidate from his Liberal Party; in other dioceses it was a virtue. There were no sanctuaries. Even Notre Dame, which was solidly conservative, was successfully sued over its burial practices. Fights were carried on through civil courts, church proceedings, newspapers, and public platforms. Ottawa, London, and Rome were inundated with cases and petitions. The civil courts remained careful and correct, they were confused outsiders. Rome was appalled. The liberals were guilty of various errors, but the fury and invective of conservative attacks exceeded all bounds of Christian decency.

Notre Dame's interior dates from this age and this fight. However, in fairness, it must be noted that Notre Dame and the "Holy War" aren't the whole story of the age. There were other churches, other political messages, other aspects of religion. In 1875 Bishop Bourget, a conservative, was building a downtown cathedral in Montreal and he wanted to drive home a point to the English. He built an exact reduced scale replica of St. Peter's, the St. Peter's of Rome, in the middle of the English business district. It was a strong message and a well made point. His cathedral still looks nice in the middle of the downtown district and, here, I have no problem with the interior. It's traditional.

There's one large picture that, for me, set the tone of the cathedral. Father Nicolas Riel, an early Canadian Martyr, is being dragged from his canoe by Indian assassins. It's dramatic and sad. Looking beyond the immediate tragedy, though, there's also the story behind the use of a canoe. It was the only way to get around in early Canada. It was the homely vessel of the Catholic clergy. This is the story of the poor and humble side of religion, generations of unremembered Canadian priests going their lonely rounds, going to death in canoes. This is what you find in the cathedral. This and a traditional interior that, as Terry once put it, is a place where she could pray,

In a sense I guess this all boils down to musty old politics and personal preferences. Terry liked to pray in familiar surroundings, and I'm looking for canoes in church. Not very weighty material there. Back to the "Holy War" and Notre Dame's interior.

Rome eventually ruled against the conservatives. They knew, they must have known it was coming. This is the only explanation that makes sense to me. They knew they were losing. And, with that, they thought the world was in danger of losing the old beliefs in an ordered universe, a universe of place and hierarchy, which would no longer be understood. There must be a place, there was a place, for a lasting record of their beliefs—the interior of O'Donnell's great church.

The guide book speaks of great artists like Victor Borgeau. It's true. It was to be expected. Conservative or liberal, Montreal likes to go the class route. But the message, the real message, is from the brilliant classically trained conservatives of the "Holy War." They poured all of their turbulent intensity into this one positive statement. It's their justification, their vision of the ultimate goal and, in fairness, I must agree that they made their point.

It's awesome, overwhelming, and unbelievably beautiful. It's a glorious blend of lighting and color—rich colors, subtle colors, blues, reds, rust, gold, walnut, pine, all the colors and shades of the palette, and all in perfect blend. The pulpit is a masterpiece. The windows, statues, and paintings are all notable works of art. Each and every pillar is a design of subtle ingenuity. No detail has been overlooked. And, up front, rising above all and containing all, is the towering center altar. This is the interior of Notre Dame, the ultimate statement of other worldly glory. It is the final conservative statement from the "Holy War."

Poking Around

These kind of things always happen when you least expect them. I was in one of the lobbies of the Place Villa Marie complex and I asked one of the workers, an older man, for directions to the Metro. He said, "I won't help you get to where you want to go." It took me completely by surprise. I retreated. I couldn't think of anything else to do. I was stung and helpless, and I'm sure it showed. He won. Now that it's all over I can sit back and grin about it. I can even wish the old man well. In his own mind he's probably one of the last defenders of the old Libre Quebec movement.

His cause seems to have gone the way of so many of the movements of the 60s and 70s. He probably hopes it will come back. I doubt it. The movements had their day. They made whatever impact they had to make and now we've moved on to other concerns. But the old man doesn't seem to have moved on. He probably dreams a lot, too, of how promising it all seemed back then.

Then, as now, the Province of Quebec was considering something called Association Sovereignty. At that time, however, rudeness was the fashion at the popular level. But this was more than just a street movement. It had early backing from several quarters. Political leaders were proposing serious changes. Respectable support came from various European and Canadian intellectuals. France's Claude Julian wrote a book to explain and defend the movement in terms of a balanced Western world perspective. Jane Jacobs, with a commission from the Canadian Broadcasting Corporation delivered a penetrating series of analyses in the 1979 Massey Lectures. She examined the Quebec proposals, and explained them as ideas that could work. But, after everyone had their say, this conservative old province voted against it. And, so far, the movement continues to lose at the polls. So now the old man works on and scores against occasional tourists like me. This has been my only experience with studied rudeness and I can't (or won't) consider any other explanation. Stand fast at your post old man.

Meanwhile life goes on in the city. It always does. While the old man was out demonstrating, the province was working through their quasi-governmental Societe Generale de Financement, to attract European industries. While the bishops were fighting the "Holy War", their favorite politician, Sir George-Etienne Cartier, was promoting railroad construction. Whatever else, it's a commercial city. It's an old fur trading town, friendly and obliging, but tough at the core. It goes with the location.

From various places in the city you can look north and see the Laurentian Hills. They're on the other side of the St. Lawrence trench. It's shield there, incredibly ancient.

We'll get to that later. The only hill here is Mount Royal. It's right in the middle of the city and it dominates everything. It's a relic of a fairly recent age, about seventy million years ago. It just sits there, high and lordly in contrast to the surrounding plain, and it's good to see how well the city has used this great landmark.

There's a "chalet" that overlooks the city from the top of Mount Royal. It's a public building with a restaurant, gift shop, and grand hall. It must be a great place for formal affairs—fancy weddings, proms, government receptions, charity balls, and things like that. During the day, though, when it's not being used for any formal affairs, it's a good place to sit, drink coffee, and just plain hang out. Even at midday it's romantic—formal hall, large windows, outside terrace, and the city spread out below.

The overlook guide arrows are a big help. They do a clever job of locating the main sights. You see McGill University with its gray gothic buildings climbing up the slope, the business district with buildings that seem to be as high as the hill, City Hall with old Montreal spread around it, the river, and fertile valley plains as far south as you can see. There isn't any northern view. I think it's because Montreal prefers facing south.

Viewed or not, there's a north. It's the shield. It's there. It's a source of business, and there's no point in ignoring it. It has good points—wilderness areas, lakes, ski resorts, timber and minerals. People live there. People live wherever roads go, but that isn't far. We'll talk about it when we get there, somewhere the other side of Ottawa. But, from here to there, it's going to continue, a dark brooding cold mass on the edge of vision. Montreal and Ottawa were built on the edge, they have the shield for a backdrop. You really can't understand these cities unless you know that.

I'm not suggesting that people here consciously avoid the shield. I'm not even suggesting that everyone's aware of it. I'm just pointing out that it's there and, because it's there, you couldn't build the city any further north. Montreal is snuggled against a northern wall. I think this has something to do with why the Mount Royal Chalet faces south.

From the chalet terrace you can see the fertile valley plain, the harbor, and the river. It's a good base—mineral rich hinterland, farm products, and water transport to the interior and Europe. All that helps explain why there's a great financial and commercial center spread out below. It doesn't do much, though, by way of explaining the charm of this remarkable city. And it's more than just a beautiful chalet. It's bits and pieces here and there all over the city. I think some kind of cumulative process is at work here, pleasant walks, flower carts, old restaurants, architecture, history that's mellowed, and so on. It is romantic.

ONTARIO

Adieu Quebec

The drive from Montreal to Ottawa turned out to be longer than I remembered. This route only covers a small corner of the Province of Quebec. My plan was to spend time in Montreal and then move on to Ottawa, but I wound up spending two more days in La Belle Province. I went to the park at Oka to see where the Ottawa and St. Lawrence Rivers meet. Next I spent some time chasing after some old Patriote history in St. Eustache and, finally, the story of some early pioneer courage at the Long Sault, what's now a little roadside history site at Carillion. That's a place where seventeen Frenchmen and one Huron Indian Chief were killed in a desperate attempt to stop about eight hundred Iroquois warriors who were intent on destroying the then small settlement of Montreal. Obviously, they lost and the Iroquois won. But the price of this wilderness victory was so high that the battered and discouraged Iroquois warriors returned home to lick their wounds, and Montreal was saved. France, Canada, and the United States too: we must never forget the gallantry and bravery of these few who gave their all so we could stay on.

That ends it though. I could easily have stayed on another couple of weeks, branched out, and followed all sorts of interests. That's a problem with Quebec. The history, sites, and customs are just American enough to be familiar, and just different enough to be fascinating. La Belle Province is a beguiling temptress, but I have to get on with my cross country plan.

Robert Mac Kinnon

My Personal Slant on Canadian-American History.

I'm going to browse around for a while on family history in New England, Maryland, and Nova Scotia. It's my background, and it probably explains something or other about how I see North American history, and relations between the two countries. Part of it is personal, but there is a good part that is straight North American history, and I'm not always sure where one ends and the other picks up.

Both sides of my family go back to the early Scottish settlers of Cape Breton Island, Nova Scotia, Canada. These hardy ancestors shared the province with a lot of equally hardy people from New England. Many of the early Nova Scotia fishing villages were set up by New Englanders who were working their way up the coast. Then, at the time of the American Revolution, there was a large influx of New England Loyalists. Stephen Laecock, a Canadian humorist, said the mix was "half Yankee Loyalists who wouldn't stay home and half Scottish highlanders who couldn't."

The Scottish Highlands? Home? That sure was a long time ago. No, home has to be on this side of the ocean. Cape Breton Island? My father left there in the 1920s; for the rest of his life he called Boston home. My mother's parents left Cape Breton Island back before 1900 to go gold prospecting in British Columbia where, sorry to say, they didn't strike it rich. Anyway, after that, they returned east, also to Boston, and raised a family.

Maryland is my home and I don't want any other. But what about those other places? They count too, if for no other reason than simply because there's comfort in knowing they're there for me if I ever want them. Home can also be a place that will take you in, or take you back. The United States and Canada both have overall good records on this score. And we are, all of us, just as entitled as my grandparents to use the whole North American Continent as home base and, if any of you don't want to, you don't have to go back east to raise a family. But my grandparents thought they did. The east coast still had a pretty strong hold on their America. But the hold was weakening. In colonial times the Atlantic Coast's hold on Anglo-America was almost total.

On Maryland's Eastern Shore—that's the way east peninsula part of the state that runs from Chesapeake Bay to the Atlantic Ocean—there's the well preserved and picturesque colonial city of Chestertown.

U. S. ROUTE 2 - CANADA TOO!

For anyone interested in such places, this is a great little walking town. If you visit you'll find historic markers telling you about how George Washington used to travel through on a fairly regular basis, and other such bits of history, all of which are true. Chestertown was an important center. As a matter of fact, according to the 1790 census, it was the population center of the United States.

Two hundred ninety eight years after Columbus landed, one hundred eighty three years after the first landing in Virginia, and the population center still hadn't gotten as far west as Baltimore. It was still on the Atlantic side of the bay, on Maryland's Eastern Shore. All up and down the east coast people were doing their level best to stay within walking distance of the Atlantic Ocean.

There was an Atlantic community. Maryland's Eastern Shore was part of it. New England was too, and it wanted to keep things the way they were. Massachusetts, for one, objected to the Louisiana Purchase on the grounds that the United States shouldn't lose its Atlantic orientation. President Jefferson went ahead with the purchase anyway, and the results were exactly what the New England orators had warned against. The United States became a continental nation. The Atlantic Ocean was no longer the dominant shaping feature of American life. This started a new pattern for the United States, Massachusetts and Maryland's Eastern Shore included.

Nova Scotia, however, along with Canada's other maritime provinces, remained facing the Atlantic Ocean, and it wasn't until the 1850s that they started thinking about joining the continent. They tossed the idea around for a few years, then Nova Scotia made a specific point of voting against it. They understood the thrust of history, America's westward push, railroads, changing transportation patterns, and, with the passing of the old sailing ships, the drop off in trips from and to New England. They considered all these things in the clear light of their bright northern days. They considered, looked east, and decided to stay with their Atlantic Way of life. They decided that, given a choice, they would not be a part of the Canadian Confederation.

The vote was overwhelming. Their provincial assembly had gone along with confederation, but the people of Nova Scotia voted to repudiate this agreement and stay out of the Canadian Confederation. Power politics was the order of the day, however, and the powers in charge decided that Nova Scotia's vote would not be considered. Nova Scotians were not to be given the choice. They were told that the British North America Act was binding, and that both London and Ottawa insisted that Nova Scotia be part of the Canadian Confederation. It was probably just as well. The railroads were opening up the interior and creating new business patterns. It was a join up or be left behind situation. And, what was more important, while all this politicking was going on in Canada, the north won the Civil War in the United States.

Malcolm, one of my Nova Scotia cousins, told me that our great grandfather, Alexander Mac Kinnon, was caught by the U. S. Cavalry in West Virginia with a string of horses he wanted to sell to the Confederate States of America. My father, Bostonian as could be, became indignant when I asked him about it. He insisted it never happened. Dad and Malcolm were both jolly family historians, and this little disagreement got to be a family joke, but neither one changed his story. I don't know who was right. However, despite Dad's Yankee pride, his grandfather was probably pro-Confederate.

Canadians overwhelmingly favored the South during the Civil War. It wasn't the slavery question, they were against slavery. It was the self rule question. Canadians had near total agreement with the states rights philosophy of the Confederate States of America. But the North won and old Alexander—if he was in West Virginia—had his horses confiscated. Tough life. The Yankees took his horses and his own government wouldn't count his vote. Neither country was fooling around and my great grandfather wasn't the only one who got the message. The British North American Colonies were going to be faced, along a three thousand mile border, with one strong unified country. Like it or not, the time had come for Nova Scotia, British Columbia, and everything in between to get together.

This doesn't mean they had to come up with some overnight national sense of unity. Their history, and their preference, was sectional. They weren't trying to imitate our South either but, at the same time, they were well aware of the word's North American connotation when they formed a "Confederacy" in 1867, just three years after our Civil War ended. The different sections more or less agreed to work together as a nation, but not at the expense of their separate identities.

It took a while for everyone to accept it as a real government, but things eventually worked out. Federal power was expanded to the Pacific, and railroad lines were completed from Nova Scotia to British Columbia. Canadian nationalism became a new force on the continent. The more important things haven't changed though. We're still friends.

We zig and zag historically, but the relationship is still about the same as the old one we had in colonial days between New England and the Maritime Provinces. We're each other's best trading partners, we're comfortable in each other's countries and, in a general sense, we're all cousins.

But that's enough family talk for now. I still haven't satisfied the problem of poor old great grandfather Alexander and his lost vote, but that can wait.

Ottawa

It must have been some notion of respect for royalty or something. The old Queen Victoria painting in Ottawa's Senate foyer has been saved from two fires, an earlier one in Montreal, and then the 1916 Parliament Building fire. The cry went up—fire—and, in both cases, someone's first thought was to save the picture. No disrespect intended to anyone's queen, but poor old Victoria would have been better off if they let the thing burn. It's a bad picture. The artist couldn't even paint both arms the same length.

Then again, I guess if you don't have a good picture, a bad one is the next best thing. Just so long as you have something to remember the old queen. She's the one who selected this city to be the capitol of Canada, at least that's what the history books say. But I've spent enough time in Government service to have a pretty good idea of what that means. She reigned. She put her name on a piece of paper and that made it official. I haven't found anything to show how much she really understood, or whether or not, in fact, she was fooled. From all accounts, though, she was an intelligent lady. She probably knew.

After all, the location was important to the British Government even before the city submitted an application to become the capitol. The Rideau Canal was completed when she was in her teens and, if nothing else, she might have remembered the bad handling of the cost overrun. The British government originally built the canal here because they needed safe transportation in a secure strategic location, away from the American border. Now it's the showplace and pride of downtown Ottawa. It provides winter ice skating, summer boating, nice wide walks, and a busy week's supply of tourist attractions. It was the impassable old Rideau River, though, that gave me a sense of the cost overrun. It's rugged. There's a big waterfall at its entrance into the Ottawa River; it's not featured but you can see it by walking to the back of the World War II Memorial Park on the Sussex Drive Bridge. Then, worse than that, there's the Hogsback—that's what its shape looked like to early settlers. It's still there, just a short scenic ride from downtown. Even with a dam, the water still splashes over the rim, speeds, whirls, and crashes against a long stretch of nasty rock formations. But this is getting away from the question of whether or not Queen Victoria was fooled.

What happened is that the town was originally named after Colonel By, the man in charge of constructing the canal. Incidentally, he deserves credit for a superb job. All of his work, especially the way he damned and bypassed the Hogsback is first rate, and the flap over the cost overrun wasn't his fault. He kept his home office superiors advised. They hid the true costs from the government. Anyway, after the work was through, Bytown was left with a lot of idle construction workers. The area reverted to what it basically was, and to a great extent still is, a lumber center. There's a beautiful river drive; no more logs in the river but, looking across, you see the Gatineau Hills, the timber rich shield area of Quebec. Then, as now, most of the lumber business was on the Quebec side of the river. There were few jobs for the construction workers in Bytown, and they became an unruly problem for the whole area.

But Bytown was here to stay. Despite unemployment and other problems, it even grew to the point where it wanted to be the capitol of the new Canadian nation. And there were some pretty good arguments in its favor. It was a central location with railroad service, and it was neutral territory in terms of Canadian politics. The argument against it was that it was Bytown. Things had really gone down hill since the Colonel left. Thanks to the antics of lumberjacks, idlers, drunks, and toughs, the town had gained one of the worst reputations in the British

U. S. ROUTE 2 - CANADA TOO!

Empire. To put it bluntly, the place was a thieving, violent, drunken, ugly disgrace. The Queen couldn't allow the prize to go to that kind of place. So the town changed its name to Ottawa, submitted its application, and became the capitol of Canada.

It was just as well the Queen did not know, or pretended not to know. Questioning Canadians, any Canadians, even Bytowners, wouldn't have been a very smart thing to do. Shenanigans aside, and so long as they weren't insulted, these people would stay proud and voluntary members of the Empire. Ontario had been founded by Loyalists from the United States, pioneer types from western New York and Pennsylvania who relocated to a new Canadian frontier after General Burgoyne's defeat at Saratoga, New York. And the Quebec French were forever trotting out Tache's proud boast, "The last cannon shot for maintenance of British rule in America will be fired by a French-Canadian hand." Everyone was pretty much in agreement with the British tie-in. So there was British allegiance—and there was Canadian spunk. British rulers always seemed to know they could rely on the one—so long as they accepted the other.

Anyway, the two always seemed to merge into a single pattern when things got rough. Allegiance is easy to understand. Spunk is the sort of thing that can't be organized or predicted. It's something that crops up in an unusual way at an unlikely time. It's unpremeditated and sometimes nutty, but it's real. Think of the Canadian bagpiper on the beach during the disastrous World War II raid at Dieppe, standing erect in the midst of battle, and playing the old tune, A Hundred Pipers. It wasn't exactly rational, but it sure must have been inspiring.

The War Museum, by the way, is a good place to get a feel for this sort of thing. On our earlier trip we found that the guards are friendly kidders. Terry commented to one of them on how realistic it was walking through their mock-up of a World War I trench. He said, "Yeah, but it doesn't have the mud and rats." She shuddered and he grinned. It's nice to find guards who kid and spend time with casual visitors. But this is just me reminiscing again, and I have to get back to the story of the city's name.

The bandy armed picture hangs on, probably hoping for another fire. Otherwise, I expect the Queen would be pleased. At least she got rid of that dreadful Bytown. There are some artsy, pricey downtown properties claiming to be Bytown reconstructions, but that's just advertising hype. This is Ottawa. All of it, even the canal, is Ottawa. Time and fashion have a way of transforming everything. In this case, it's for the best. The planners have made pleasant use of the natural setting, rivers, islands, cliffs, and canal—and they've added buildings and monuments with just the right touch of dignity. And, as the guidebooks say, the prevailing architecture is Victorian.

It's a comfortable and friendly city with good downtown strolling areas. As always, though, you have to be especially careful in unfamiliar places. There are a couple of places where they actually seem to aim their cars at tourists. I've been told that my attitude is narrow minded on this matter; the drivers are aiming at all pedestrians, not just tourists. Either way, be careful, watch the kids, and follow the cross walk rules. Beyond this, and for all its other places which are open and friendly to tourists, it's still a good idea to keep in mind that this is a proud capitol with its own way of doing things.

A friend who worked in the National Archives Building in Washington, D.C. once told me of a couple of portly women, obviously tourists, who walked into one of their larger business offices. This, of course, was when I was still working, back before the terrorist threats. The ladies stood there, looked around, and one said to the other, "Oh, nothing here but a bunch of government workers." Then, without any sign of embarrassment, they turned around and walked out.

Those ladies might have been embarrassed if they came to Ottawa. Back then, Canada was stricter than us when it came to visitor control in government buildings. Who knows, though, maybe the ladies would stay with the tour and not have any problem at all. When they got through with the Parliament Building tour, they could walk over to the commercial Sparks Street shopping mall—it's only a couple of minutes away—and behave like paying customers. Or they could spend their time on a big farm that's inside the city limits. It's an experimental place where the Agriculture Department works on northern crop development, and even spends time figuring out how to make farming areas look more attractive. There's livestock too, but it's some Museum people running that part of the show. It's well worth the short drive but, again, follow the rules, especially around the animals.

Anyway, the point is that Canada has a long record of enforcing control in government facilities. For the most part it's a simple matter

U. S. ROUTE 2 -CANADA TOO!

of common sense and respect, but I think there's also some caution that dates back to the 1916 Parliament Building fire. The Centre Block of the compex was destroyed, and a Parliamentary investigation came up with reasons for suspecting arson. The case was never solved, and it took Canada until 1922 to complete the basic rebuilding. They're still sensitive about this horrible waste of a national treasure.

Fortunately, however, everything wasn't lost. The staff closed the iron doors and the fire didn't destroy the Library of Parliament. For the most part, what you see on the tour—chambers, lobbies, and the Peace Tower—is relatively new. It's a good tour, interesting gothic architecture, wonderful exhibits, and a good view from the top of the Peace Tower. It's the old library, though, that's the high point of the tour. Just being allowed inside that magnificent building is a privilege, especially for me.

On this and previous trips I've been more or less following lumber trails and old lumber rivers all the way from Maine to here. Its been the same story all along the road. The lumberjacks moved in and cut down the white pine trees. The virgin growth is gone. The lumber lust of the past has become a legend. Part of the reason for this lust became clear when the guide ushered the tour group through the library doors. The whole place—foyer, balconies, even hand carved decorative plaques—is pure white pine from Canadian forests. It's awesome. There actually seems to be a rich warm glow from the wood. We were only allowed to stay in there for a couple of minutes; members were using the library. But I saw enough. Now I understand why the virgin white pines were hunted and cut.

The Parliament tour should complete the stay in Ottawa, but I still have my Nova Scotia concerns. I can't leave yet. There's no getting the horses back, but great grandfather Alexander deserves satisfaction for his lost vote. And this is on my conscience because, after the tour, I came out and admired a statue of Sir John A. Macdonald, the builder of Confederation. How does a descendant explain this to a Nova Scotia ancestor? Tell you what Alexander, I'll drop the title and we'll just call him "John A." That's what everyone else seems to do. Besides, we don't want to show too much respect for someone who treated Nova Scotia that way.

Honestly, though, Alexander you wouldn't believe some of the anti-Confederation talk coming out of Quebec since then. A person would think they were the ones who opposed confederation in the first place. We know better. John A., and that big handsome Frenchman from Montreal, Cartier, they're the ones who set up Confederation. They carried their provinces. They insisted Nova Scotia had to stay in despite your big vote against it.

Now we have John A.'s statue in an honored position in the big circular drive. But, to be fair, there's a lot come out in history books since your time Alexander, and I guess it's up to us to try to understand. As near as I can figure it John A. didn't really ignore your vote. He just didn't accept it. He had some old lawyer arguments, besides he needed time to make the thing work. Anyway, there was no way you could beat him in Parliamentary proceedings. No one could ever do that. And even you would have to agree he made the thing work. Another thing you'd probably agree with is that it's an honest statue.

They didn't try to make him look handsome. He's standing there, like always, with a thin face, receding hairline, big nose, and the start of a smile. You can see that in the old pictures too. What the heck was he always smiling about? They say he was some kind of a cut-up with his own crowd, but you wouldn't know anything about that in Nova Scotia. I think your group knew more about the big forehead. That's where you can see some frowning, and a lot of determination and intelligence. The smile must have been friendly though. Despite all the fighting and attacks, he really wasn't vindictive. He just kept on smiling, fighting, winning, and building Confederation.

Sorry Alexander. The longer I look the more the smile seems friendly. And we must remember that the man used his great powers and abilities for a good cause. He was dedicated to Confederation and Canada. He put it together and he kept it together. He built the railroads, and he made it work. Just standing here and remembering all the fights makes me think he had more pure steel in his spine than there was in all those miles of railroad tracks. I've changed my mind. I think I'll go back to calling him Sir John A. Macdonald.

But let's you and I try again Alexander. I've only got so much time to spend, and I'd like to feel at peace with your spirit befor I go. Maybe if we go to another part of the complex. The circular drives in this place are so peaceful and sedate, it would lull anybody into accepting anything. I think they plan it that way, historic buildings, big shade trees, river overlooks, and wide lawns. It's nice, but let's go

U. S. ROUTE 2 -CANADA TOO!

out front, near where the outside street traffic is, and look at the statue of Sir Wilfred Laurier.

Now there's a man for your liking Alexander. He was a French-Canadian who opposed Confederation, but he came around. He accepted. He grew with Canada, and Canada grew with him. I know about some of the problems. British assumptions, American tariffs, provincial demands, western dissentions, eastern sulks, the Quebec Holy War, and railroad politics. But Prime Ministers always have to work with those kinds of things. That's government. We're talking about something more important.

Don't get me wrong on this though. I'm not disparaging government. After all Sir Wilfred was Prime Minister for fourteen years, and he was good at the job. In a sense, too, I guess he was lucky to have this for his homeland. Being Canadian was a novel idea, but most people were willing to give it a fair try. All they needed was some good example, some reason for pride. They got more than they bargained for.

You must have felt it Alexander, even in far away Nova Scotia. Some of it can still be seen in the statue, the graceful bearing, and the gentle wise eyes looking out from a noble face. But, for all the statesman like quality, he still looks like he would step down and start fussing again if he saw a single Canadian child in danger. Rarely has any government been headed by a person who grew so in love with his own people, all of his people.

There's your satisfaction Alexander, Sir Wilfred Laurier, the man they call the First Canadian. The man? The First Canadian and the country that grew along with him. The simple genius of the Canadian solution turned out to be confederation with diversity, and Sir Wilfred Laurier showed how attractive it could be. No one stopped being what they were. At the same time, though, with him as an example, everyone grew proud of being Canadian.

There. Now I can go on with the trip. I can leave Ottawa knowing everything is as it should be. I've convinced myself that Alexander accepted the results, so I'm at peace with him. Queen Victoria can be proud of her signature; Ottawa grew up to be the beautiful swan of world capitols. Sir John A. Macdonald can go on smiling, the provinces are still playing a rough game of politics, but confederation stands. And they've put Sir Wilfred Laurier's statue out by the traffic so he can spend forever looking out at the people he loved

Robert Mac Kinnon

The Canadian Shield

The farm areas were giving over more and more to the forest. Then, after Petawawa, the lands started rising and I was back in the Shield. Unmistakable. You can see it. You can sense it. The soft contours are gone. The land is rough. There are rock outcroppings and there's a change in the forest. The birch trees are still around. The birch and, a little farther west, the aspen, seem to thrive in this northern struggle for existence. They grow tall and thin, and they seem to be the only broadleaf trees in an evergreen forest. The conifers, pine, spruce, and so on, have taken over most of the land. This makes for a darker forest.

The big geography book I used to brorrow from the New Carrollton branch library said the shield was a little more that half the land area of Canada. The Canadian Government pamphlets say it's a little less than half. Both agree that it spills over into a few parts of the United States. The name, incidentally, only refers to its shape. It's widest in the north, up by Hudson Bay, and It's not quite as wide in southern Canada. Think of the shield shape of a policeman's badge. Roughly, it's shaped something like that. So much for the shape. It's big. It's spread right across the middle of Canada, and a good part of the geological data is still in the guess category. Earth sciences can be more accurate when they're dealing with times that had life forms.

At one time a leaf falls. At another time a shellfish dies. The form of the leaf and the shell of the fish leave imprints in soft deposits of mud. Mud hardens and those shapes become captured imprints in rock. These are the historic indicators of life and cnanges in the land. The leaf shows the type of tree that grew before the formation of the rock layer. The shellfish indicates that water covered the land before the formation of another rock layer.

Science is sophisticated in these areas. It can trace changes in life, and the earth around it, back to about five hundred and seventy million years ago. The time is divided into ages, and the oldest, the one that goes back all those years is the Cambrian age. This is the earliest time that life, and it's only a few simple forms, can be recorded with any regularity.

It gets more difficult when you try to go back further in time. Scientists keep going after it but, in most places, it's not a subject with popular appeal. There's no reason why it should be. Most of the United

States, for example, isn't pre-Cambrian. There's some spillover from the Canadian Shield, some pre-Cambrian basement rock in a few canyons, and other occasional outcroppings here and there, but nothing really to attract popular interest. Most of us are still trying to understand the land forms of the last few hundred million years. Our own country wasn't here before that. As it turns out, though, it's an add on to something that was here way back when.

The Shield is pre-Cambrian. It's the original North America. This is the great rock mass that gradually rose out of the ocean well over a bilion years ago. It's the oldest part, the ancient core of the North American continent. It was here then, and it's here now. The newer rock formations, the additions of the past few hundred million years, aren't dominant, not up here. Pre-Cambrian is still dominant.

It's real. It's more than just a geological cataloging exercise. It's a physical barrier and the historical experience of Canada. The Indians, French, and British, each in turn, learned about the shield. They learned there were restrictions on where they could live. Southern Ontario, the St. Lawrence Valley, and the western prairies were fine. But, in between, and to the north, was a great land mass not fit for human habitation.

The restrictions lasted until recent times. That's part of the story of why Sir John A. Macdonald became so immersed in railroad politics. The western provinces are the other side of the shield. There were no roads. Canadian commercial routing only went as far as the Great Lakes. From there travelers and goods had to go through a part of the United States. In one instance Canada even had to ask permission to transport a military expedition to the west. It was an impossible situation. Regardless of cost, the shield had to be conquered.

Now there are railroads, roads, and a few small cities on the shield. There's even some farming. The growing season is short but some clay beds, relics of long forgotten lakes, are fertile. There are lonesome stretches of road; the population is still small. But, overall, the traveling is easy and the accommodations are just fine. It's deceiving though. That's still a rough wilderness out there. The maps show it. You can see it from most of the higher elevations. You look out and realize you're on a thin macadam strip that's been forced through an immense wilderness.

That wilderness started pre-Cambrian, and its been scoured clean of life time and again by great glaciers. It's too large an area to perrmit simple description. Textbooks, and government pamphlets divide it into different geological provinces according to this, that, and another type structure. It doesn't really matter. They're all pre-Cambrian; they're all harsh. There's muskeg, swamp, thin acidic soil, trees, and rocks. There's a rugged beauty in many parts, but I can't help but think of it as cosmetics, a thin covering over rocks. Sometimes the rock surface shows. Most times it's just below the surface. Its been there through more than a billion years of change, and its hoarded great stores of mineral wealth. But, apparently, its still resisting the changeover to life on the planet. It's pre-Cambrian in origin. It almost seems to be pre-Cambrian in preference.

Voyageurs

Ontario put up a roadside history marker to let us know that the Ottawa River took its death toll. Mattawa has markers to show the canoe routes. About ten minutes past Mattawa the Samuel de Champlain Voyageur Heritage Centre has a good replica of one of the great voyageur canoes. Then, just as you enter North Bay, there's a big roadside map sign which shows where the voyageurs had to "portage"—carry the canoe and contents. There are many reminders.

Mattawa is where the Mattawa River enters the Ottawa River. That's the whole point of the location, the joining of the rivers. It's a good little browsing town, parks, the rivers, a great array of eight foot high wooden statues, and historic plaques honoring the voyageurs. It's a good lunch stop too. Just before you get into town there's a nice hillside restaurant that overlooks the Ottawa River. I got a window table and spent my time looking across to the high hills and wilderness on the Quebec side. A railroad bridge crosses the river but that seems to be the only sign of civilization over there. The maps don't show any towns or roads. All I could see was the hills, and the Ottawa River coming from the north, a north I'm not going to see, at least on this trip.

Mattawa is where the road turns west. Mattawa has always been the turning point. This is how you get across this part of the shield. You follow the waterways, the Ottawa to the Mattawa, the Mattawa to Lake Nippising, cross the lake and follow the French River to Lake

U. S. ROUTE 2 - CANADA TOO!

Huron. There, now you're out of the dreaded shield and into the great American center. Lakes Huron, Michigan, and Superior are spread out before you. There's no end to the places you can go. The hardest part was finding a route across the shield.

The French didn't discover it. Their Indian allies showed it to them. Nothing changes. We all follow the same route when it's our turn, Indians, French, British, Canadian road builders, and now me. This is the old water route to the upper Great Lakes. This is why the French were all over the Midwest while our own American colonists were still huddled along the Atlantic Coast. This is why Montreal was a great fur trading town.

At first it was the western Indians coming along this route to Montreal's annual fair. Before long, though, French explorers had penetrated through to the farthest end of these waterways, and beyond. They started out looking for a short cut to China. They succeeded in dotting the Great Lakes area with fur trading posts. Buffalo, beaver, muskrat, otter—countless millions of pelts came over this route.

It was the animals, of course, not the Indians who were the innocent victims of this trade. The Indians were willing participants. So long as the supply lasted, they were in a good position to bargain for European products—guns, ammunition, utensils, steel knives, blankets, and, yes, booze. Our own government, and all of the others, tried at one time or another to ban this last item. There was never any real success. The French even referred the question to some Paris theolologians. The answer came back that it was a mortal sin to provide liquor to Indians. It would be interesting to see a theologian trying to explain that decision at a tribal council. Anyway, furs were big business and, thanks to the voyageurs, Canada got its fair share of the trade, and then some.

There's no way anyone can visit or consider this part of the continent without getting around to the voyageurs, the hardy and courageous canoe-men, mostly from the Montreal area, who became a legend in Canada and Midwestern parts of the United States. Their skill and endurance was phenomenal. They could handle any type canoe. They were the ones, probably the only ones, who could stand up and pole a canoe through rapids. Their specialty, though, was the big Montreal canoes that could carry about four tons of freight.

The portages were swift. They never faltered in carrying heavy loads through mud, swamps, or over hills. Once back in the water, they'd sing in unison to keep the rowing rhythmic and fast. It only took them about two months to go from Montreal to the farthest end of Lake Superior.

It must have been impressive, the sound of song and the steady beat of oars coming across the water as the great canoes raced furs to the Montreal markets. It's easy to imagine the scene with so much wilderness still around. Maybe I'm romanticizing the whole thing because I'm viewing the river from restaurant windows and my own little walking tours. I don't think so. I know, too, about the sadness of the Ottawa marker reminding us of the death toll. It's an appropriate rememberance. But, for all the harshness and danger, the voyageurs were a happy and proud group. They were the masters of these wilderness waterways.

North Bay

North Bay is the perfect example of why there are no perfect examples. It's shield with nice farming areas. It has a direct line to the Artic. The railroad runs from here to Moosonee at James Bay, the lower end of Hudson's Bay. But North Bay isn't north. It's Midwest. It's all a matter of how you see things.

On the road I've been following this place comes across as a soft spot on the edge of the shield, a soft spot with a Midwestern town. There's nothing like a big lake and good clay farmland to encourage a lasting settlement. There's no feeling of isolation, separation, or invasion of wilderness. There's no reason for the people here to think shield or north, unless they want to. With good roads and Toronto at the other end, this is part of Ontario's great farming and industrial complex.

It might have been north if Sir Wilfred Laurier hadn't decided to open the north by building a railroad up there too. But that's just my impression after talking to a young clerk in the railroad station. He obviously couldn't understand my preoccupation with the north. No matter, he was polite and he went out of his way to be helpful. He even rummaged around to get me the pamphlet on the Polar Bear Express to Moosonee, but he acted as if that was someone else's territory. Why didn't I consider the "Dream Catcher Express", a seasonal excursion trip they run around this area. It's too late in the year for the Polar Bear Express, but there's still time to sign up for the Dream Catcher Express and the scenery is spectacular. Yes, I could get connections from here to the Polar Bear Express, but the real starting point is Cochrane, up at the northern cross Canada railraod. Why not take both pamphlets. Sure enough. Thanks.

I went back to the motel, read the pamphlet, and daydreamed of a low cost summertime excursion to the Artic. The young fellow probably went home and told his wife about the confused Yankee. But I'm not the only one who's confused. The pamphlet's fare schedules and text say Cochrane, but its route map shows North Bay as a connecting point. At least the mapmaker seems to see some logic in including North Bay as the other end in a run from the Hudson Bay area.

So far as my immediate plans go I know none of this matters. I won't be able to take the Moosonee trip, at least not anytime soon. But that still leaves me with the question of the young fellow's attitude. I guess I can see his point of view. Yesterday, when I drove out of the harsh terrain, I found myself in a typical Midwest setting—town, a strung out busy Main Street, traffic, farms, railroads, industry, and the clear waters of Lake Nipissing. Toronto is just a couple of hours or so down the road. The north is way up there with the second railroad. Who am I to argue? But when I drive out of here tomorrow, I'll be back in the northern shield.

Sudbury

Might as well get the bad story out of the way first. There was a time when this place could have been listed as Exhibit "A" for environmental damage. And it was something they did themselves. Over and over again heaped up tons of ore were roasted until, finally, the sulfur content caught fire and burned itself out. Year after year the stinking, smoking sulfur laden fumes blew off to cover the east. Trees, bushes, grass,—just about every living thing died, and the landscape turned grisly black. They've done a remarkably good job of greening up, but you can still see some patches of black hilltops along Kingsway 55 and other local roads.

What happened is that nickel was discovered in some ancient lava flows. It's more than just nickel. There's iron, copper, silver, and platinum. The Sudbury basin is incredibly rich in many things. But the story on the earth damage is nickel—nickel, greed, war, American capital, Canadian politics, indifference, inefficiency, and the pressures of the times. Too much happened in too short a period of time.

There were earlier surveys indicating valuable ores in the area, but they were ignored because commercial mining wasn't practical this far into the shield. All that changed when a railroad construction crew rediscovered the wealth of Sudbury in the mid 1880s. Then, seven years later, Europe succeeded in developing a nickel-steel alloy for use in armor plate. The international armaments and greed race was on. A French company tried to keep the monopoly on the nickel-steel alloy development, but that didn't last long. Canada had Sudbury and the railroad. It overwhelmed all opposition and, going into World War I it controlled seventy percent of the world market.

Competition, indifference to a newly opened remote area, the pressures of war needs—there are many excuses. And, without question, the nickel ores of the Sudbury Basin were a mainstay of the free world's production during both world wars. Then too, the argument can be made that this was an isolated case and not really representative of Canadian development. After all, this is the province that won twenty-one prizes for its educational exhibits at Chicago's 1893 World's Columbian Exhibition. And that does it for the bad story.

Now for the good news, and it is very good. With full cooperation from industry and government, the clean up and greening resulted in a rebirth of nature in the Sudbury Basin. Considering the extent of the prior damage, this was a truly remarkable achievement. And they didn't stop there. This is still a business town with mining wealth and, so long as they were at it, they went ahead and built nice new buildings in the downtown area. Then, and again I think it's related to the scientific aspects of mining, they became an important part of the space program. This is a modern "with-it" town.

With all this I have to remind myself where I am. There are a few roads connecting a few communities and providing access to the rest of Canada; otherwise, this is all wilderness. This is still the shield. Local companies are still running sea plane service with bush pilots who know the territory. And the best place to get a fix on this is the popular Science North complex. There is an admission charge, but it's worth the price. They give a good feel for the bush pilot business; the complex includes 2 billion year old rock formations; and they have space program exhibits which feature Sudbury's contributions. This sure is a with-it part of the shield.

Departure

Shades of the old movies, Gene Autry saved the day. Somebody or something had to save it. It was off to a dreary start and it sure wasn't going to save itself. That's one of the problems of being alone in the car. When I get down there's no one to lift my spirits. Fortunately, this doesn't happen too often. But it happened when I left Sudbury.

I thought it would be easier to just drive out and get breakfast somewhere along the road. It turned out to be a long drive and, the more the road went on, the more depressing it got. There's no explaining it. It just happens. And the shield didn't help. In fact, I thought this was the roughest section of shield I saw. It seemed like mile after never ending mile of up and down lonesome road with dark forests and rock outcroppings, ahead, behind, and on all sides. Maybe it was the shield telling me something—telling me I don't belong. That's the way it felt. Maybe it was too long a wait for breakfast. I finally found a place.

It was just a truck stop, nothing particularly cheering, nothing depressing either. There were a couple of travling families, a couple, and a few truck drivers. It was company. It was enough to make me start feeling better. Next came the warm food. Then, with volume up, the restaurant radio blared out with Gene Autry's "Back in the Saddle Again." How is it possible to get a warm nostalgic feeling for something I never cared that much for in the first place? I don't know. At times, though, Autry can do what the Boston Symphony never could do. He can make you feel the lonesome moods of America and let you know you're not alone. So I got seconds on the coffee and went on enjoying the warm pleasant restaurant.

The sun was brighter when I came out, the hills looked lower, and the shield was just another place with a lot of trees. The Canadians are right. Never mind pre-history and geology books. The shield can be tamed. They're doing it. Elctric wires and roads span the area. Sudbury and the mining towns to the north are old hat by now, and the Polar Bear Express runs all the way to Moosonee—at least in the summer.

Meanwhile I drove on out. Once I got breakfast out of the way it didn't take long at all to get to the soft rolling area of Lake Huron's north shore. I saw an oak tree, then another, then they were commonplace. I was back in a familiar mixed forest setting. There were glimpses of the lake, open grassy fields, long views to the horizon, and restaurants about fifteen minutes apart. I thought I left the shield behind. Maybe not yet.

About a mile and a half up the hill from Desbarets, right beside a protruding rock formation, there's a little pull off area and a sign. The Province of Ontario wants us to know that the ripples in the rock were formed about two billion years ago.

I only acknowledge that in passing. It's just some kind of a leftover, a reminder of what's behind. I'm in Great Lakes country now, and on my way to Sault Ste. Marie, not the nice city on the Canadian side, the nice city on the American side. That's the history I've been reading. But no goodbys to Canada. I'll keep in touch.

MICHIGAN

Sault Ste. Marie

It's all about ships. The Corps of Engineers set up the information center. Tourists can go there to find out about the ships, the locks, the Great Lakes, and so on. The Corps got everything right on this one. They even have a big chalk board, behind the information counter, showing when the ships are going to be passing through in each direction. The park and the fountain are nice too, but that isn't what its all about. The big ships are the attraction. This is manly stuff and it's amazing, after seeing a few ships, how we all manage to sound like authorities.

This morning I was up and out at about six a.m. A fellow from the other side of the motel courtyard was walking his dog. What woke me was a ship horn with a different sound, and I had just done a fast job of getting dressed so I could rush out in the direction of the locks. I just barely saw the end of the ship as it cleared the lock. It was a big one, though, and I think it was flying a Russian flag. The fellow with the dog said he didn't see the flag, but it looked to him like an ocean going freighter, and he guessed it was carrying grain. I was tempted to get my binoculars and drive Artemus down River Road to see if I could get a better look while the ship was still in the channel. But then I figured that, by the time I got organized, the ship would probably be gone. They travel pretty fast. Besides, there'd be more ships to see during the day.

The ships are on the St. Marys River. It's really just a spillover. So long as Lake Superior keeps its present tilt, the excess water buildup will continue to spill out on this end. If the tilt changes, it might start spilling out on the other end, at the St. Louis River over by Duluth. Then the drainage would probably be south to the Mississippi instead of east to the St. Lawrence. But, for now, the drainage is on this end. The water leaves Lake Superior, rushes over some rapids, and goes into Lake Huron.

It's just a shallow river, and it isn't a great drop, only about twenty-one feet. But it's swift and over rocks. Historically, it was a tough old bottleneck. There are stories of voyageurs shooting the rapids. Some of them probably did when the water was high but, even for them, that wouldn't have been a normal practice. The St Marys River, Sault Ste. Marie, the Soo as it is generally called, was a portage.

Lake Superior with so much of the west on one side. Lakes Huron and Michigan with the American and Canadian Midwest on the other side, and all cargo had to be carried along the banks of the St. Marys River. You could only have as much business as could be carried overland. One of the Montreal fur companies built a canoe trench along their side of the river, but we knocked that out in the War of 1812. It was retrenched after the war, but it never worked right. The Soo was to remain a portage until 1855.

For such an out of the way place it was a pretty good portage. Right through into the 1840s it got its share of the fur business. But it was still frontier, an isolated semi-wilderness that was just about totally cut off in winter. And, as happened in many of the frontier posts, these conditions attracted ambitious individuals, driven men, leaders who knew how to cope with the wilderness and get the job done. Up here it was Henry Rowe Schoolcraft. He was a man of many accomplishments and he did try hard, maybe a little too hard, to be great. His main claim to fame is the discovery of the true source of the Mississippi River. However, after the discovery, there was a nasty public squabble with Lieutenant Allen, the officer who headed the military contingent on the expedition. It wasn't over credit for the discovery, no one disputes that. But Lieutenant Allen made a case that, in his pell mell rush to get back after the discovery, Schoolcraft's negligence jeopardized the lives of the soldiers. Also, on a very minor matter, Schoolcraft tried not to give credit to the Reverend Mr. William T. Boutwell, who was also on the expedition. Boutwell told him that the Latin words for "true head" were verITAS CAput. Schoolcraft combined parts of these words to come up with the name

Lake Itasca which is, in fact, the true head of the Mississippi River. It wouldn't have hurt to acknowledge Boutwell's contribution.

So Schoolcraft was imperious, and maybe even jealous. He was also talented, efficient, and good at playing the role of the great white father. You can still see his big white house on River Road. It's beside his father-in-law's smaller house, and they've been spruced up. His place must have been an impressive landmark in the semi-wilderness that prevailed here in the 1830s. He was a Government Indian Agent, and effective at it. He knew how and when to live and act in the grand style, and how and when to travel in the wilderness, and how and when to awe or be pals with the Indians.

This is a digression and I don't want to stray too far from my interest in the waterways, but I've always been astonished by our mixed bag approach to Indian dealings. Not, mind you, that I'm talking of anything that could be called bad intentions. Schoolcraft, for example, was a sincere friend and promoter of Indian understanding. His wife was half Chippewwa Indian, and his writings on Indian lore were so well accepted that Longfellow borrowed from them to write the poem Hiawatha. And yet, none of these family and humanitarian interests interfered with his duties as a Government agent.

Oficially, and Schoolcraft worked on this, the Lake Itasca expedition was made in an attempt to keep the lid on a Chippewa-Sioux war. Along with this, the routing was planned to include the discovery of the source of the Mississippi River. And, by way of service, the party included a doctor who vaccinated the Indians, a misister who gave them the word of God, and a military officer who studied invasion routes and made note of the number of warriors at each Indian camp. But all this is a different and more complex part of the old history, and I'm not going any further with it. My concern is still with the waterways.

The expedition to Lake Itasca, of necessity, was over the waterways—paddling and portaging all the way. That was the only half way reliable way to get around the Midwest in those years. We tend to forget the enormous change brought about by the railroads. They could trunk and branch through just about any terrain. Weather was almost never a problem. Freight and passenger arrangements were organized and efficient. Service was safe, reliable, on time, and relatively cheap. And they could keep building on year round service and volume. The more business they got, the more they could compete on rates.

New traffic patterns were set, and they changed the face of the nation. The railroads could, and did, ignore the old water routes, they could, and did, build in whatever cross-country direction suited their business and construction needs. Turner, an historian of the frontier, quotes an unnamed writer whose main complaint seems to be that the railroads built from the east. The railroads, according to this writer, "succeeded in reversing the very laws of nature and nature's God—rolled back the mighty tide of the Mississippi, and its thousand tributary streams, until the mouth, practically and commercially, is more at New York or Boston than at New Orleans."

Regardless of direction, the simple and casual old days of water transport had to give way. They couldn't compete. And some good things were lost forever songs of the voyageurs, wind in the sails, and funny stories about farmers trying to herd hogs down a muddy bank and across a gangplank. There was no place left for small loads, rowing, portaging, and waiting for the wind. And, on most rivers, there was no reason to carry on the old struggle against eddies, currents, and shifting sand banks. Gone too was the thrill and agony of watching until a sail appeared on the horizon, or of listening for the horn blast of a steamboat, and then voicing the ultimate satisfaction—thank God they made it. But all is not lost.

The horn blasts are here. The big ships are back in control up here. Locks were built at the Soo, and big ships handle the bulk transport. Some of the literature says it is the world's busiest waterway, some just say that it exceeds the tonnage of the Panama Canal. Whatever the statistics, it's busy. And the old dangers are still here too. These are inland fresh water oceans and, for all the pretty paintings, the lakes are still a harsh northern challenge, even for modern ships. There's ice through about five months of the year, storms are sudden, and the turbulence has often been deadly. But the lakes are still the key to the treasure. They're still the low cost water route to the iron and copper mines, and the grain fields of the west. So this is the place where inland shipping survived. The big ships are here to stay.

The cameras keep clicking. The Corps of Engineers built a long high public viewing platform so tourists can watch the passing ships. Another big one is coming from the Superior side and it has to stop right in front of the platform. Ropes are thrown out. The ship towers about twenty feet above dock level. The gate closes behind it. The water level goes down. The ship sinks until the deck is a foot or so below dock level. There's a big horn blast, and the ship sails out. Then the show goes on again with a ship going in the opposite direction. This one will reverse the process as it rises to about twenty feet above dock level. It goes on like this all the time. I do my best to see all the ships listed on the chalk board, and I'll get up again at six a.m. if I hear another different sounding horn. This is manly stuff.

Fort Michilmackinac

According to the road signs, the new Interstate Route 75 and Route 2 are the same road through to St. Ignace. Actually, it's a modern super highway and I didn't take it. I mapped my own course from an old WPA travel book and followed the old roads—what used to be Route 2. The old roads are more relaxing and enjoyable. But the new road is a good thing too. It connects the two parts of Michigan, and that's a big improvement.

Water's the problem. Until the new road and connecting bridge were built, there was no direct land transport between the two parts of Michigan. Ferries ran in season, but they could never handle any real volume. People in the southern part of the state were pretty well cut off. They had year round access to places like Detroit, Toronto, and Chicago, but they couldn't drive up and enjoy the sights of their own upper peninsula, the Soo, old missionary graves, different terrain, waterfalls, natural curiosities, off-shore resort islands, lakes, rivers, and great expanses of wilderness. And, of course, this works both ways. I'm back to following an interest in some early colonial history, and I needed the bridge to get to what I wanted to see on the opposite shore, the other side of the Straits of Mackinac, Michigan's historic water obstacle. It was nice to be able to cross with ease. The Straits of Mackinac have finally been tamed, but it took a long time.

These Straits are the connecting water link between Lakes Michigan and Huron, and they weren't bridged until after World War II. Actually, it's stretching a definition to call anything up here a strait. That's a wide and rough water expanse between Michigan's two shores. People say it's a strait because they want to say Michigan and Huron are separate lakes. The reverse could be just as well accepted, the combined area could be considered one huge lake. Anyway, there's a bridge now, and it leads to one of the finest archeological reconstructions in America, the old fort at Michilmackinac. It's exact and accurate even to having the old British flags flying from the flag poles.

Michilmackinac was originally one of the fortified French trading posts that dotted the wilderness in an arc that extended from Montreal, through the Great Lakes, and down the Mississippi River to New Orleans. There was the usual European understanding; discovery and and exploration conferred ownership. Internally, though, the French weren't the masters of this land. They were trading partners and allies of the Indian nations. That was an arrangement that worked well enough until the French left.

The English-French battleground was in the east, not out here. But the Indians from these Midwestern areas helped their French friends. Then, after France was defeated and withdrew her armies, the Indians were alone. Alone, that is, with the English, the nation of settlers. And there was no clear understanding of the rights of either party.

The Indian side of the story was that the land west of the English settlements was the hereditary homeland of independent tribes, and not the property of any European nation. The English side of the story was that the land, from the settlements through to the Mississippi River was English; they won it from the French. And, along with all this, it should be understood that the land was a virtually vacant wilderness.

Any one of the medium size cities in this state has more people than the total Indian population in these old French territories at the time of the transfer. French explorers would travel for days without seeing any humans. A few hundred Indians on an island, or in a village on a river bank and, for thousands of square miles, the land was theirs. Their settlements would relocate up or down river, or to a different island, but their range didn't include the interior. They lived in small numbers along the water concourses. The interior was visited by hunting parties, otherwise, it was unoccupied. This was the forest wilderness.

The victorious English entered this land and, with a civilized grace that disgusted the Indians, the French surrended every single

U. S. ROUTE 2 - CANADA TOO!

fort. The French traders, who had settled around the forts, stayed with the understanding that the English would permit them to continue in business. This was their livelihood and they had no place else to go. But the soldiers packed up and returned to France.

Now the forts blonged to the English. The Indians were no longer respected allies of a European power. They were subjects, children really, of a new great white father, the King of England. No point in consulting or reviewing an English-French treaty with them. They couldn't read it and, anyway, they were just subjects who came with the land. They'd have to do as they were told.

The Indians couldn't read the paper, but they could read the portents. They knew they were few, while the English were many. They knew that the English considered themselves to be masters of this land. And they knew that, once the settlers started to fill in this wilderness, the Indian way of life would disappear. They knew, and for all its primitive harshness, they loved their own way of life in this wilderness. They knew all this, and they were ready to follow the gifted leader who organized their war against the English.

The leader was Pontiac, an Ottawa chief down the lower end of Michigan, near Detroit. But his location doesn't matter. He was the trusted one, the planner, the leader, the inspired orator who, for the rest of his life, was revered by the Indian tribes. He spoke. He sent out the word, and they acted.

This, once again, is Francis Parkman's version, and I know some later historians think he overstated the importance of this one leader. But all the essential facts are right, he told the story well, and, as usual, although I don't mind his English bias, I think he could have moderated some comments. He understood Pontiac's love of the wilderness, and he gave fulsome praise to his intelligence and organizing ability. But Francis also considered it necessary to render harsh judgement. Pontiac is called a thorough savage and "the satan of this forest paradise." That means that Pontiac led the resistance to civilization. It also means that settlers were tortured and killed.

The frontier erupted. Pontiac's call to battle was answered by Ottawas, Chippewas, Pottawattamies, Sacs, Delawares, and Shawanoes. Even some of the Iroquois Confederation—the Senacas and Cayugas—joined in the attacks. The forts at Detroit and Pittsburgh held out, but they were surrounded and isolated.

Otherwise, the Indians captured all of the frontier forts. The settlements, especially in Pennsylvania, were ravaged. Hundreds were burned out, killed, captured, and tortured. Fleeing refugees poured back to the safe eastern areas.

By this time the so called English settlers were a mixture of English, German, Scots-Irish, Dutch, and other nationalities. But, so far as the Indians were concerned, all settlers were English. Only the French were spared. They were the old allies, the trusted friends, and there was still hope that the King of France would wake from his long sleep and send another army to punish the English.

The remaining French, who were still mostly around the forts, were sufficiently knowledgeable and informed to know in advance that the attacks were coming. They weren't, however, a part of the conspiracy. Some even tried to warn the British, but their advice wasn't heeded. Worse still, their motives were challenged. Captain Etherington, the commander of Fort Michilmackinac, saw the warnings as French attempts at trouble making. He threatened to arrest and deport anyone who continued to report such stories. After that, the French followed the only course open to them. They stayed neutral and kept their scalps.

Captain Etherington lost the fort to Indian trickery. In response to their invitation, he was outside watching an Indian ballgame. At a given signal, all the Indians raced through the open gate, killed the few soldiers who were in a position to offer resistance, and took possession.

Etherington, another officer, and eleven soldiers were held prisoner, eventually released, and returned to Montreal. They were well treated, probably because their original captors gave them over to another tribe. But, despite Indian torture practices, kind treatment wasn't unusual. The general rule with the Indians was that they would torture some prisoners, after a battle, when emotions were still aroused. After the torture lust passed, the remaining prisoners would be treated, like Captain Etherington and the other survivors, with kindness.

There were other soldiers, however, who were not so fortunate. Twenty-five British soldiers were killed here. Some of them were victims of the Indian torture lust.

The war, if it can be called that, lasted less than a year, and the ending wasn't dramatic. The British rallied, relieved the forts at

Pittsburgh and Detroit, penetrated deep into Indian territory with superior numbers, and forced Pontiac and the other chiefs to sign new treaties. In the overall sweep of history, this can't be regarded as anything more than a minor event. Most people don't even know that it happened and, considering the numbers, that's understandable. There were a few dozen British soldiers at each of the isolated forts that were spread almost halfway across the continent. There were a few hundred Indians, here and there, attacking the forts and burning the settlements. And there were the poor suffering settlers who were burned out and forced back east.

But you can't stand on the ramparts of Fort Michilmackinac and regard it as an unimportant war. This was a critical British outpost and, even now, you still get some sense of isolation. Looking to the west you see a wide expanse of Water and Michigan's forested upper peninsula. Pontiac went to war for this. Pontiac and his Indian allies fought, to the best of their ability, to keep this a wilderness. And, to the end of his life, Pontiac insisted that he only recognized English ownership of the forts, not the land. Even in defeat he didn't give up his claims. No wonder the Indians loved him.

Looking to the east, however, you see the straits, Mackinaw City, and the bridge. Great modern ships ply these waters—some from as far away as England—and they are carrying cargo to and from cities like Detroit and Montreal. I see houses that remind me of New Carrollton. Looking overhead to the bridge, there are trucks carrying goods to market. I see a stream of cars and I know they are filled with people like me. This is America. This is our civilization and part of the price was the lives of those twenty-five dead and forgotten British soldiers. Michigan is more than just archaeologically correct. It is right to keep the old British flags flying over this one piece of land.

The Upper Peninsula

How to satisfy the Michigan Territory? That was President Jackson's problem in 1836. No matter how good its legal claim, The Michigan Territory couldn't extend to a line the Congress had originally drawn from the southern tip of Lake Michigan. That would have included the city of Toledo with its fine natural harbor on Lake

Erie. Ohio, which was already a state, insisted on having the city of Toledo, and Ohio had the votes and political muscle to enforce its claim. The solution: give Michigan the Upper Peninsula and, for an added sweetner, dangle about $400,000 in front of them. That was it. Take it or leave it, but no Toledo. Michigan didn't like the solution, territorial opinion was strong on that matter. Accepting the northern wasteland in place of Toledo was a bad bargain. It was that or nothing, though, and, anyway, they sure could use the $400,000.

So Michigan got stuck witht the Upper Peninsula. It really was a wasteland, a small portage at "the Soo," a few fur posts, and a lot of wilderness. No one could blame them for being disappointed. They couldn't even get to the place. An argument could be made that there were two ways to get there overland. Actually, for all practical purposes, there were none. One overland route would have been through a large part of Canada, but that was foreign and mostly wilderness. The other would detour the traveler through three other states, Indiana, Illinois, and Wisconsin. The only real way to get there was by boat, and that only in good weather. Winter was a time of near total separation and isolation.

Now there's the bridge across the strait, and the new Interstate Route 75 runs through to Sault Ste. Marie. That gives a pretty good year round link to the rest of Michigan, at least for the eastern end of this huge peninsula. The separate world of the Upper Peninsula reasserts itself, though, after you drive just a few miles west of the bridge. It's still a place of long distances, small population, and local concerns. But, at least it's no longer a total wilderness.

There's industry. Some of it's natural to the area. Some is just people's determination to have a reason to live here. This has been going on for a long time. Over the years they've used hardwood blast furnaces to manufacture pig iron. They've had mining booms, especially during war times. There's still some open pit mining north of Route 2. Otherwise, the mines are inactive now, but they'll come back. They always do. Meanwhile, most of the iron and copper lies undisturbed, a natural strategic reserve for America. There were tremendous lumber booms when the Midwest was opening up and also, of course, when Chicago had to rebuild after their great fire. Escanaba and other port cities shipped out millions of board feet of prime lumber and, as usual, the white pines were the first trees cut.

Forest industries are still here, and there are several large pulp mills. There's light industry, quarries, year round tourist activities, casinos, some commercial fishing, and some farming. But the population stays small, and it's mostly concentrated in a few cities.

Escanaba has an industrial section, a good size active downtown area, deep water ore shipping docks, nice looking residential neighborhoods, marinas, and parks along the lakeshore. Norway and Iron Mountain are especially pretty little cities, off to themselves and surrounded by hills. Iron Mountain lost the mines but gained a pulp mill and, just recently, a junior college. It is doing well and you can still hear some British accents there. A part of the population is descended from miners who were recruited from Cornwall, England when the mines were opening up. Manistique is getting some benefit from a couple of local casinos. It's all interesting, but there are just a few cities. Wander away from these and you might bump into a black bear. Most of the land still belongs to the forces of nature that created it as an immense and isolated land mass between two of the Great Lakes.

The first white intrusion here was French and absurd, but it is not fair to blame them for that. Christopher Columbus showed Europe that the world was round. If anyone sailed west they should wind up in China. And there was no way logic could deduce there would be another continent, and a second and even larger ocean in between.

The logic of the situation was that China should be somewhere in the neighborhood and, in keeping with diplomatic norms, one should meet the host government on its own terms. Strange as it now seems, the French were only being correct when they traipsed through here with Mandarin robes and other Chinese trappings. It wasn't their fault that the Imperial Court was another eight thousand or so miles to the west, and this place had a different set of attractions.

Some of the trees along the Lake Michigan shore have been shaped—distorted actually—by storms. Conditions in late fall and winter are frequently harsh. But nature seems to compensate in other seasons. In good weather the southern and eastern parts of this peninsula are a smiling land, a place to hear Whitman's "cheerful voice of the public road." It's bright and cheery with long vistas, empty beaches, sand dunes, a deep ravine with nature walks, woods, rivers, picturesque waterfalls, and friendly restaurants.

Whitefish is advertised everywhere, "pasties" signs become more frequent as you travel further into the peninsula. The fish is a northern Great Lakes delicacy, popular but local. Attempts were made to market them nationally but, as it turned out, there isn't a sufficient supply. Now the rest of us have to come up here if we want to enjoy the taste. Pasties, the other food, is a spiced meat pie that was brought over by Cornish miners. They'd take these heavy pies down in the mines and, when lunchtime came, they'd have a meal that was filling and still warm. They're delicious but, after having pasties for lunch, you'll have no appetite left for dinner. They'll never go over in diet conscious America. Back to the fish.

Incidentally, unless you actually go fishing up here, the closest you'll get to live fish is a commercial trout hatchery in Watersmeet. It was closed this time around, but I understand that is only temporary. On a previous trip we found their food dispensing machines, ten cents for a small fist full of pellets. Terry and I used up all our dimes, and we alternated between throwing a couple of pellets at a time and throwing fist fulls at a time. It didn't matter. The fish, especially the bigger ones, kept darting in and snapping up everything that landed on the water. They'll be caught after being released but, as usual, you have to know where they are before you can catch them.

The lone fisherman on the bridge down by Port Inland told me the fish weren't running well. In the few minutes I was there I did see one trout flopping along over the rocks. But that is probably a poor location. I saw more fishermen at other locations and they seemed to be doing pretty well. Just outside Escanaba I saw two burly men who were struggling under the weight of all the king salmon they caught. The fish were strung from a heavy pole and, one man on each end, they kept stumbling and pausing as they carried their heavy load to a pickup truck.

So much for fishing, natural beauty, good eating, and the wholesome enjoyment of innocent outdoor pleasures. They're here. Other pleasures have been here too, indoor pleasures that weren't so innocent. So far as I know, though, this is just past history, and it's only concerned with the western part of the Upper Peninsula. And, even at that, most of the action was in the town of Hurley, which is on the Wisconsin side of the border.

This western end of the peninsula is an ore rich, heavily forested shield area that's spilled over into the United States. The town grew here because of the ores and the mines, but the miners were mostly family men. The lumberjacks, almost all single men, the old crews from New England and Canada along with a lot of new Swedish and Irish recruits, were spread throughout the deep remote forests of this typically rough shield area. It's back again to geography, history, and our old philosopher friend John Dewey, but this time we get Hurley.

Dewey said, "Festal celebration and consumatory delights belong only in a world that knows risks and hardships." He wasn't talking about Hurley and lumberjacks, but it fits. There was more than enough risk and hardship in the isolated lumber camps. With Spring, and a pocket full of winter wages, lumberjacks were pleased to find a town that offered festal celebration and consumatory delights. Hurley had it all, all the drinking, gambling, and other delights that any lumberjack could want. It was famous in its time.

The stockade's gone now. That was a place where customers had to pay to go in when they wanted to be with the consumatory delight ladies. I walked around and I very definitely did not see any fine buxom ladies prancing around in tights, singing, dancing, pushing drinks, and promoting a general air of festal celebration. In fact, Hurley's famed old Silver Street looks like a normal, passed over, slightly seedy business street. There are a few old saloons left, and they are advertising exotic dancers. I guess they are trying, but it's no stockade. However, the street did make a splashy comeback in prohibition days. Who knows? Maybe it will again when times become more festal. For now, though, the Upper Peninsula seems to be a place for outdoor pleasures.

WISCONSIN

Ashland

Its been a pleasant two days in a smiling land. The only sour note is me. I planned my time to end the day with an afternoon trip to Madeline Island, and a truly horrible old story. But that's some musty old reading. It can wait. Right now I'm wondering how long Ashland can stay off by itself as a nice little city.

Keep saying the same thing for about a hundred years. Don't worry if it doesn't happen. Just don't change your story. Keep repeating it for another hundred years if you have to. Someday Ashland's going to be a big city with commercial interests all over the map.

It's going to happen. Ashland has railroad service, and the commanding spot on Chequamegon Bay. It's an ideal harbor, big sheltered bay, deep water, and islands to serve as breakwaters. It provides sheltered mooring with access to the markets of the world. From here you can have water transport to the eastern cities of the Great Lakes, or, through the St. Lawrence Seaway, to the oceans of the world. But, so far, no one has met the challenge of finding a use for this tremendous harbor

They've tried. The ores from Michigan's Gogebic Range, some of the closed mines I passed in the Upper Peninsula were shipped through here. But the real boom in ores was a hundred years or so ago. Following that, there was a lumber boom, the usual northern pattern, with the usual emphasis on white pines, and now it is settled down to a couple of pulp mills. Some brownstone deposits were quarried—from the peninsula that runs along west of the harbor, and the islands at the other end of the bay—and shipped for building material. All this

U. S. ROUTE 2 - CANADA TOO!

past business is enough to explain the fine old homes in the residential areas. Otherwise, it has little to do with today's Ashland.

The harbor sits there in great empty splendor, and the city's settled down to ignore the next hundred years of waiting. They might be surprised. I don't have a crystal ball, but there's a development somewhere along the line, and it has to be more than just a return of the ore business. The day is coming. It's just about inevitable. It's a rich land, and it's just a question of time. They'll be a use for the great harbor. But, for now, Ashland can ignore it.

For now the city's sitting off to the side, like any good little Midwestern center, and minding its own business. And apparently the empty harbor, and even Route 2, don't count for much in the scheme of things. They don't seem to belong. In fact, it's Route 2 that runs along by the harbor, and neither one seems to have much connection with the city. There's an overlook of the harbor. There's the usual busy highway lineup, motels, restaurants, gas stations, and stores. That's it, just a drive through place with the amenities of the highway, and a big bay off to the right. Nothing to connect the traveler to the city.

Main Street's just one block behind Route 2. It sits there and provides a different set of stores, gas stations, and restaurants for the locals. The signs in store windows feature local activities and events, and there are interesting paintings on the sides of several buildings. A few blocks further in I found the nice old houses, and watched some kids walking, clowning, and chasing their way to school. This city's a whole world away from international harbors and interstate highways.

So they choose to live and do local business away from the harbor and highway. Okay. Maybe they can go the better part of the next hundred years keeping it their own little city, a home town, but a friendly home town. Main Street's typically Midwest—casual, comfortable, and a good place to have breakfast. And breakfast's important. People watching at Midwestern breakfasts is one of the delights of the trip.

One thing I've learned in the Midwest is to look for big old Main Street restaurants, the kind with plain furnishings and hot coffee in mugs. That's the place to go for breakfast. It's a place, and a time of day, when it's natural and easy to be relaxed. It's a place where people can eat, and start the day on their own terms. Some eat alone and read a newspaper. Some just sit alone, usually in a booth. Some socialize at tables where regulars keep coming and going, one leaves, another takes the seat, and there's no break in the banter and conversation. There's buzz, bustle, warmth, privacy or sociability, comfort, and seconds on the coffee. It's a simple meal, but there's a good human rhythm.

Anyway, breakfast was in a big old Main Street place that's both a café and an ice cream parlor and it was nice. The Northern Great Lakes Visitor Center, also on Route 2, is one of the best take ins in the Midwest. And the peninsula that runs along beside the bay is one of the prettiest places on this route, apple orchards, woods, and the little jumbled resort town of Bayfield. I even saw an old abandoned quarry, small but grotto like, on the way out. It's in a recessed area in the side of a hill, a murky pool at the base, and the whole thing almost completely hidden by trees growing in front of it. Very pretty, everything here's very pretty, especially at this time of the year.

Madeline Island

Now we get to the real point of this side trip, which is to see Madeline Island, and get on with the old story. As it turned out Madeline Island is a popular spot for local tourists, and there was no indication that any of the tourists, other than me, was aware of the old history. I shared the ferry boat ride with a bus full of senior citizens, and they thought this was one of the better parts of their tour. I talked, too, to a young couple who were going to peddle their bikes around the fourteen mile island. They think it's an exhilarating place, and they're right. All the tourists are right. Madeline Island is a lot of nice things. It is not a cursed place.

All the wisdom of Hollywood to the contrary notwithstanding, there's no such thing as a cursed place—I hope. I still sit up occasionally to watch late night horror shows, but I don't really believe them. Some innocent exposes a grave, or fumbles with the wrong artifact, or something, and wicked spirits are released to corrupt and enslave the souls of the living. Oh, if only we we had left well enough alone.

Oh, if only we can keep those fumbling innocents away from Madeline Island, Wisconsin. The curse stories go back a long way here. Schoolcraft and his party knew something about them. The Reverend

Mr. Boutwell even joked about Lt. Allen having slept overnight on the island. But a better source for what did, or didn't, happen is the writings of William Warren, a gentle, half Chippewa Christian historian who lived around here until the middle of the 1840s.

The island was originally a protected homeland for a local band of the Chippewa Nation. After receiving guns from the French, they abandoned the island, and drove the enemy tribes, the Fox and Sioux, further south and west. But this may not be the exact sequence of events. Whether they got the guns first and then abandoned the island, or abandoned the island and then got the guns isn't known. In any event, they left the island and wouldn't return. The question is why? Possession of guns only explains their success against other tribes. It doesn't explain a rejection of their island home. There's no real answer. It's a mystery.

Large parts of the history are sketchy. The events on the island happened about two hundred years before Warren's time. By this time the Indians, or at least some of them, had moved back to the island. But they were still native enough to have the old traditions, and Warren drew on these to write an Indian version of the history of the Chippewa Nation. But sometimes, as in the case of the island, he had to rely on other sources.

Warren, who was on good terms with the elders, never completely got to the bottom of the matter. This was one subject the elders refused to discuss. Warren went on to pick up horrible, but apparently true, bits of stories from old traders, and half breeds. There were tales of cultism and strange evil rites, of men dressed in bearskins, people being poisoned, grave robbing, cannibalism, and the return of dead spirits. Something, probably something violent, happened. There seems to have been some sort of strong rejection of evil practices, abandonment of the island, and silence. Warren confronted the elders with these stories and they refused to comment. But Indians avoided the place and then, as if in fulfillment of a curse, the whites came and suffered a cruel fate.

Sometime around the 1600s the French came and built a fur post on the island. The Indians visited to get trade goods, but they wouldn't live there. The post was run by a manager who lived there with his wife, their two small children, and one workman. The workman murdered the husband, wife, and children. He did it in early Spring when there was still too much thin ice for him to escape, so he hid the bodies in a pile of rubble. That much is clear. There are differing stories on the order in which he killed them, and the motive. It might have been theft but, more likely, he attempted to rape the wife.

When the Indians came the murderer told a plausible story about the family having left, over the winter ice, to visit nearby Indian camps. They were presumed to be lost. Then some French officials came for a spring check, investigated, found the bodies, and arrested the murderer. After that the story gets confused again. There are three versions of the ending. The first is that the murderer was returned to Montreal and executed. The other two versions have it that he escaped and sought refuge with an Indian tribe, probably the Hurons. In both endings the Indians killed him in disgust after he bragged about his foul deeds. In one version an Indian brave immediately tomahawked him. In the other version the Indians sat him down to a feast, stationed an armed brave behind him, and told him he would be killed when he was through eating. The poor wretch ate as long as he could, then the tomahawk descended.

Jim, Cal, and Superior, Wisconsin

The James J. Hill bust, old Jim Hill from the shoulders up, is back home. It's on railroad property—his railroad—and they built a big new pedestal for him with an American flag on one side and a BASF railroad flag on the other. For many years before this his bust had been in front of the old Central Junior High School, but they tore the school down, and there's nothing there but a vacant grassy lot. All things considered, that didn't seem very respectful. I'm sure Jim expected better.

In life Jim was an advisor to Presidents, or at least to President Cleveland. Well, maybe not that much of an advisor, but he knew Cleveland, and he supported his policies. It's hard to sort out some of these things because Hill's "authorized" biographer went in for a lot of puffery. Anyway, things were better in Cleveland's time, the days before Theodore Roosevelt and his government crew interfered in Hill's business dealings. Not that they did any lasting harm. Jim Hill could always find another way to do what he wanted to do. Besides, he sincerely believed that the Sherman-Anti-Trust-Act wasn't intended for railroads.

His railroad pioneered the Route 2 course I'm going to be following from here through to the Puget Sound in the State of Washington. He built the business, he knew the business from the ground up, and he didn't like interference. So far as he was concerned the railroads, his and all the others, were about the best thing that ever happened to America. He actually told people that, "It is not an exaggeration to say that in the past history of this country the railway, next after the Christian religion and the public school, has been the largest single contributing factor to the welfare and happiness of the people." You have to wonder where motherhood, family life, the Constitution, and a few other things would have fit into his scheme of values. But, for sure, his number one value message was plain—leave the railroads alone and they'd do right by the people.

Another thing, too, about the old school is that it did serve as the White House for a while. It must have pleased Jim's spirit when he saw Calvin Coolidge come up the walk to set up a Presidential office in that school. Now there was a president who knew how to keep his nose out of things that were the proper concern of business. And, all the time he was there, Coolidge did nothing that would disturb the spirit of Jim Hill.

It wouldn't be right, though, to say that Coolidge did nothing— or did nothing Presidential while he was there. He signed papers and kept in touch. He approved sending Secretary Kellogg to Paris to sign a good intentions pact on outlawing war. He even gave up fishing long enough to give a speech defending the pact. He cooperated with the photographers when they posed him on the schoolhouse steps with candidate Hoover. He couldn't take the time to actually talk to Hoover, but the pictures came out fine. And every so often he gave soothing reassurances on the economy. Prosperity was here to stay. Keep cool with Coolidge.

America loved it. Coolidge, in his final year in office, accepted the invitation of Wisconsin's Senator Lenroot, and the vacation use of an estate on the Brule River, which is about twenty-five miles east of here. From the middle of June through to the second week of September, the President was gone fishing. The American system was working. We were the country that could get by with a minimum of government.

All that we needed was a President with intelligence, morals, and the good sense to let the market place follow its own natural laws. When Congress was out of session, the job could be done on a part time basis from a schoolhouse office.

So the school is gone and that doesn't bother me that much; it was just a convenience, a necessary place to do business. But it would seem right to put a bust of old Cal in front of a Post Office or some other Federal space.

On my way here I stopped in the town of Brule, had a nice lunch, walked in the wayside park, and saw the river. It's pretty, but narrow, shallow, wooded, and almost hidden. It wouldn't even be noticed on a casual drive through. And, again, I'm sorry to say, the signs in the park don't mention Coolidge. They do a nice job of covering geological history, French explorations, local Indian wars, and fishing rules—but no mention of Coolidge. And all this, of course, is just me talking, not President Coolidge. He had his own agenda. He knew what he was doing. He was enjoying nice climate and excellent fishing.

That's another thing Jim Hill would have liked, promotion of this area for its climate and bounty. He did a lot of his own promoting along these same lines, all the way from here to Puget Sound. And, to keep a good thing going, Coolidge would have approved of the way Hill built and ran the railroad—big, solid, efficient, and profitable.

So far as I know, though, Coolidge didn't spend any of his vacation time trying to understand the Hill empire. I made a start on it, but I didn't stick with it. I went out to Wisconsin point just to look across the water and see the dock that Hill built. Last I heard, it was listed as the world's largest iron ore dock. It's huge, but there wasn't any activity so I spent my time enjoying other things. It's a beautiful peninsula that's been preserved in a natural state, nice woods, beach, a lighthouse, and good views of the lake. I decided it was better to walk on the beach than go on looking at an iron ore dock. Coolidge would understand. Hill wouldn't.

That's another place where the biographer led people astray. He romanticized Hill. He made a big point of Hill being able to quote Burn's and Byron's poetry, some old lines he learned as a schoolboy. True or not, it didn't have any bearing on Hill's adult life. The truth is that, with him, everything was numbers, facts, and efficiency. He was the first to put numbers on railroad locomotives. Before he came along they had romantic names, just like boats. But Hill wanted numbers. If he had any romantic notions he invested them in high priced European paintings. Anything he spent on business, or the prairies, plains, or mountains that fed his business, was for investment purposes. The west was pure economic geography, and Byron and Burns had no place in Hill's public life. It's enough that he built an efficient railroad, kept the rates low, and gave some sensible talks.

Incidentally, his bust was in front of the school because of the talks. It's something he started late in life. He'd accept invitations, and give good strong talks at places like county fairs. They read like his legacy to the customers of the west, good advice from a tough old businessman who understood the territory. Keep the railroad grades low, it saves on engines and fuel. You can still see miles of wooden trestle bridges running over this area to give a gradual rise to the dock areas. Keep business healthy, balanced, and moving from both ends of the line; empty freight cars add to the cost. Prepare for the day when iron and other natural resources are depleted. Practice scientific agriculture; farmland can be saved for future generations. And, with all this sensible public speaking, Hill came into his own as a man who deserved to be admired for his successs, a good example for the school children.

MINNESOTA

Duluth

John Masefield once wrote a poem about a would be artist who signed up as a crew member of a clipper ship. He wanted to get a working level knowledge, and paint pictures of the moods and colors of the sea, something no one else had ever been able to really capture. He fell from the mast during a fierce storm and died. So there's a sad old story about another loser being destroyed by the sea.

There have been other artists, real artists, who painted sea scenes. Whistler, for one, did a nice job of painting ships. But that's more the romance of man and sail. it's not the same thing. In Winslow Homer's picture, *"High Cliff, Coast of Maine"* you can almost feel the coldness of the water. Even so, even with Homer, and you can especially see this in his beach scenes, the white breaking water looks more plastic than liquid. Again, it's not the same thing. Masefield's challenge was to paint the sea.

Maybe someone has succeeded against this challenge, and I just don't know about it. If so, I wouldn't be at all surprised to find out it was someone from Duluth. The town has a good record with challenges, and it loves the water. It's jaunty, like a sailor, a city in the center of the Midwest, serving the plains and prairies, but doing it as a great seaport city with gulls, docks, waterside restaurants, and all the rest of it. It has the feel and appearance of its own unique position as the westernmost port serving the Atlantic trade.

This port started with a challenge. It started by literally clawing its way to the sea. There was enough water, and a good sheltered harbor, but the only entrance was on the Wisconsin side of the border.

U. S. ROUTE 2 - CANADA TOO!

Complaints were made to Washington when the original residents started digging their own harbor entrance. With that, the whole town turned out, with every digging tool available, and the sea-trench was completed before the stop work order arrived from Washington. Now, after a long and colorful business history, it's a great port, the terminus of the Great Lakes, and the farthest inland city with accesss to the Atlantic Ocean.

The next challenge was to build on the hill that rises behind the harbor, and, from a purely practical point of view, this doesn't make much sense. It's steep. It seems that it would be too steep for a comfortable city location. Even today you have to wonder about things like pushing baby carriages, or breaking the car when there's snow on the ground. And it all seems to be unnecessary. There was no need to force all those houses and businesses onto a hill. There are perfectly good level plain areas to the south and east. But Duluth went with the challenge of the hill.

They blasted. They worked their way up the hill, building on every spot carved out by the old glacial sea. They blasted some more to get roads and railroads. Then they carved more places out of the tough old volcanic hill. Everyone wanted a view of the harbor and sea. Now they're happily perched, street after long street, row after row, practically all the way up the hill. Only the very top is left, an ancient high water level reserved for the Skyline Drive. They built that with overooks so the rest of us could see too.

As always with port cities, though, the first and final challenge is the sea. There's a good Seamen's Memorial Statue on Barker's Island on the Superior, Wisconsin side. And, of course, the sea is Lake Superior. Gentle water, Cleansing water. Water that washes the shore with soft waves. Water that reflects the blue of the sky. Water that glistens in the sun. Water for pleasure boating and commercial sailing. Water that serves the needs of cities, commerce, and agriculture. Water that gives life. Blessed water. Murky water that depresses the spirit. Water that churns in response to rain. Water that rises. Water that surges and batters the coast with great crashing waves. Water, the sailor's grave. It's not our element and, on a regular basis, it can be counted on to do its terrible worst. But, oh, what a sight when it's not acting up. The views from the Skyline Drive are magnificent. By day you look down and see the city, the harbor, and the bright blue sea. On a clear night you see the glittering lights of the city against a dark water backdrop. And the close-up views are splendid too. The sea rolls gracefully and shines and ripples in the crisp northern sunlight.

So Duluth insists on living within sight of the sea. I've seen some bright days here and understand, or, at least I understand part of it. I've seen the sea, too, when its acting up ugly, but that's the sort of thing I usually manage to avoid. Masefield, our poet with the challenge, knew a lot about bad days with the sea, but he was like Duluth. He was known as a lover of the sea. I expect that's the answer to his challenge. Love. The sea can only be understood, and perhaps painted, if you love it in all its moods. That's why I have confidence in Duluth.

The town's in love with its own environment. It loves the sea, and it loves its own old hill with a commanding view of the sea. It shows in everything, and it shows well. After all, when people go to all the trouble of building in the wrong location, just for the view, it figures they'll build with a pleasing style. No wonder it's such a satisfying place. They built to enjoy their own surroundings.

It's the overall effect of a harbor city climbing up a hill that's so picturesque. It's the setting and what these people have done with the setting. The harbor, the Skyline Drive, and other attractions are open, fun, and good places to tour. Downtown has pleasant surprises. The main library, for example, which occupies one long block, is an attractive building, streamlined, and rounded on both ends. It's the shape of a modern ship. And there are good trips that can be made outside the city. There's a grand drive along the northern shore, and, south of the city, there's the Jay Gould Park for anyone who wants to see a great river in a natural setting. And, so far as I'm concerned, the Eastman Johnson paintings and drawings of the Chippewa Indians are Duluth's family jewels. But check first to find out where they are. Last time they were in the old depot; this time I found them in the Tweed Museum of Art at the University of Minnesota, Duluth.

Eastman Johnson and the Chippewa (Ojibwa) Indians

Sometimes a picture can say more than a thousand words. Sometimes it can say things that mere words can never say. A picture or, as in this case, a group of pictures can pick up parts of life—people, people doing things, and their surroundings—with so much accuracy and understanding that we can look at the pictures and our feelings tell us we're seeing something true and human. We don't know the people. We know we'll never know the people; their lives are private. We see that in the proud character of their bearing. But we see them in their everyday activities, and we see them with each other, and we see the faces with the play of human emotions and human sensitivity. It's a quiet little set of pictures, but they're a genuine introduction to another world. We always knew these people were real, but that wasn't enough. The pictures make us feel their humanity.

Our painter, Eastman Johnson, wasn't alone in his admiration of the Chippewa people. As a matter of fact, the Chippewas were great admirers of themselves. Warren, our gentle half Chippewa historian from Madeline Island, tells about Indian legends, early contacts with the whites, and wars with other tribes, sepecially the Sioux. What comes out, along with a lot of good tribal history, is some proud boasting. The Chippewa, in addition to being better fighters than anybody else, were also better looking than anybody else. In fact, according to Warren, at least one of the wars was caused by young Sioux women looking at Chippewa men with "wishful and and longing eyes."

Longfellow went along with this. Schoolcraft fed him the old legends and then, in the long Hiawatha poem, we have still another Sioux woman falling in love with a Chippewa hero. Modern scholars say the Hiawatha story was really a tale that originated with the Iroquois Indians, and Schoolcraft was confused. He probably got the story from his Chippewa in-laws, but it doesn't matter. All the tribes swapped stories, and each group wound up taking over the ones that fit their own view of themselves. The Chippewa view was that they were a handsome people. Who's to argue? There's a long list of early white witnesses that agree with that view. Johnson took a whole summer to paint and draw their pictures, and it wasn't for our viewing. It was his own private pursuit of beauty.

There's a whole big question about that summer, though, at least to me. It's ingrained. I've spent most of my life being a father—the head of the family. I have a problem with the thought of Eastman Johnson roaming around Duluth's north shore and up as far as the

Pigeon River during the summer of 1857. This is not what could be expected of him. He came from a well connected Maine family, the kind that was able to help with some early Washington introductions. As a young untrained artist he did some fine portraits of John Quincy Adams, "Dolly" Madison, and other national celebrities. His talent was phenomenal. But, even so, his family wasn't rich, and he wasn't financially independent. Commissions—paid work—that's what was important.

Mind now, I'm only drawing on my experience as father of my own family, not as Johnson's father. The biographers don't record what he said. However, before coming out west, Eastman did manage to spend a few years in Europe studying the masters. His mother died just before his return, but she must have lived long enough to be pleased with some of the stories that were filtering back. They were calling him the American Rembrandt. Someone even said he was offered the position of court painter in Holland.

But study time was over. Money was running low, and it was time to settle down and go back to serious work. There was no need for another long vacation. He'd had his time in Europe, and he had already spent the summer of 1856 with his married sister in Superior, Wisconsin. Now he had the offer of a commission. Henry Wadsworth Longfellow who, incidentally, completed the Hiawatha poem just two years before this time, wanted paintings of his three young daughters. Longfellow was an important and influential person, and an early patron of Eastman Johnson. He deserved consideration. It was bad judgement to turn down that kind of an opportunity just to spend another summer on a strange frontier. Eastman should have been in Boston during the summer of 1857.

It took another year but common sense finally prevailed. Eastman returned to the work that suited his training and family background. He went back to doing first rate genre paintings, and portraits of the rich and famous. And, for almost fifty years following that one lost summer in the Duluth area, he was one of the most successful and popular artists in America. It was a long life. He painted portraits of the sixth and twenty-forth Presidents of the United States. And it was a good life. From all accounts he was a very decent and agreeable sort of fellow. He was well adjusted, successful, and popular. He was where he belonged, or at least where he belonged for most of his life.

After seeing the Duluth pictures I'm just about willing to suspend parental judgement, but only for that one summer. Otherwise, I still think parental judgement is a reliable guide. That one summer's the exception, however, because there was something strange about it, something beyond my understanding. It was as if some governing Indian spirit, a Mantu as they are called out here, took possession of Johnson and his talent. A Mantu could be expected to do this sort of thing, especially if it was to leave a record of the beloved Chippewa people. There definitely was something private about Johnson spending that one more season in Minnesota. I just don't know what.

Once in a while the small exquisite pictures would be taken out of his portfolio and shown to a close friend. One of his friends, a leading critic of the time, gave them high praise and tried to get Johnson back to that sort of work. But, no, that was a closed chapter in his life and, for as long as he lived, the Duluth pictures were never exhibited or offered for sale. They were private property, something he had done for his own reasons, his own record of the summer of 1857.

After he died the pictures were bought by Richard Crane, a Chicago philanthropist and donated to the City of Duluth. The display is beyond me. I stare at the Indians, they stare into their own time, and there is so much to try to understand. The time was just three years after the land, from Duluth north, had been given over to white occupancy, and I think I see puzzlement on some faces. But the old Indian way of life, with canoes and teepees is still in full swing, and the people haven't lost any of their handsome self confidence. The girl with the decorative neck band and half hidden head band is exceptionally pretty, but she looks more like a study than a girlfriend. I don't know why he was so private about the pictures. I don't know, either, why the pictures are so evocative. Maybe a Mantu is involved. And, as everyone knows, if one of those creatures feels he's being pushed too far, he can become spiteful, and do terrible nasty things. I think it's probably just as well that I drop the whole matter right now.

Morning Breaks

So far as I'm concerned, fast food chain restaurants are a great American institution, not for the food, although that's better than the critics think, but because they provide one of the uncomplicated simple pleasures of life. They're neat, clean, and convenient places where travelers, business types, and neighborhood people go for mid-morning coffee breaks. Everyone gets up and makes their own start on the day's business. Then, after the first seventy miles, after the school buses have gone, after the breakfast dishes are done, after the morning news and talk show, after the gardening, after the first calls have been made, after whatever it is that started our private day, it's off to the world of commerce, coffee, and people for our break. And, no matter what part of the country I'm in, there seems to be some sort of repeat patern to these breaks.

It's retired people to the rear where we can sit, daydream, and watch everyone else. The well groomed ladies who look like librarians, and the men in rumpled suits who look like salesmen, sit up front, one to a table, and take turns with the complementary newspapers. The librarian will have some friendly chat with the restaurant workers before she leaves; the salesman will spend a few minutes writing things in his notebook. In between we have the neighborhood mothers with their pre-school tots and infants in strollers. The infants enjoy all the surrounding motion, and the shiny plastic colors. And it is obvious that the well behaved tots have been waiting all morning for this—an outside snack, relaxed mothers, and the company of other tots—what a treat.

Fast food restaurants have earned their place in the community. They're bright cheery places, convenient for occasional meals, and a pleasure for in-between snacks. For the mealtime crowds its eggs, pancakes, hamburgers, chicken parts, and salads. For the mid-morning regulars it's clean rest rooms, snacks, and the pleasure of a relaxed break.

Hibbing

Terry and I came up here on an earlier trip. There was a big discussion over morning coffee. Should we or shouldn't we travel about fifty miles north of Route 2 to see a big hole in the ground. It would be interesting. It's on the Mesabi Range, and it's billed as the world's largest iron ore pit mine. Then, too, it seemed to fit with other parts of the trip. The northern ranges are the source of the iron ores that helped to make Duluth and Superior such great shipping centers. And it would give us a final glimpse of an old friend. The Mesabi and Vermillion Ranges, the great iron ore producing regions of northern Minnesota are a spillover, a part of the Canadian Shield that's on our side of the border.

On the other hand, we thought there'd be little to see—cold weather country, more shield, and a few small towns where the people would be ethnic something or others. That kind of thing doesn't appeal to me, especially when it's advertised. I have limited patience with my own ethnic. Other people's ethnic bores me. It almost always boils down to cooking and amateur handicraft displays. After about fifteen minutes I begin to feel like an outsider. Both Terry and I were happier with our own interests. But we had some time to spare, and nothing to lose. Might as well go. It would be fun to see the hole in the ground, and we figured we could make it back to Route 2 and some sensible accommodations before nightfall.

It's not quite as bad as it used to be, but I still hold to the notion that there's a conspiracy to keep tourists like me out of northern Minnesota. The least of it usually shows up around February. The TV announcer says, "The coldest recorded spot in the United States last night was Hibbing, Minnesota, where the temperature dropped to—-—." This is never offset by reports of the beautiful crisp Fall days in this part of the country. I guess that would be asking too much. But those silly weather reports aren't the worst of it, not nearly. One of my favorite authors, Sinclair Lewis, is the worst of it. He was a real discouragement.

Vida Sherwin, a character in Lewis' novel *Main Street*, is the all around satisfied Gopher Prairie type. She's a nice lady, and it's easy to believe in her acceptance of the town. She had bad experiences elsewhere. She "taught for two years in an iron range town of blurry faced Tartars and Montenegrins——." I'm not sure I know what Tartars and Montenegrins are, but I get the idea. Real foreign foreigners, probably surly. And I'll bet their kids are blurry faced too.

Then the United States Steel Company came out with something called "The Iron Range Answer to the Inscription on the Statue of Liberty." The thing was actually put on a plaque as part of the bicentennial celebration. The foreigners were talking back, and

U.S. Steel was their spokesman. I have to say I liked the part about them carving out "The greatness in Iron that spells America." But I didn't like the part about them being "the homeless tempest-tossed immigrants." And they keep going on with this sort of thing.

Being ethnic seems to be some kind of a promotional idea up here. One nice lady was telling me about some ethnic days celebrations, and she volunteered that she's German. Of course, she feels bad about not being able to speak German, but that died out with her grandfather's generation. Enough.

Fun's fun gang and I'm glad you're having a good time. But February isn't tourist season, and those occasional freak weather statistics are just a thing to break up winter tedium. The rest of us have ancestors from all over the place too. You're not German if you don't speak German. Ethnic celebrations are just a grown up excuse for playing make believe. And Terry and I almost missed getting to see the range and the real Hibbing.

Incidentally, anyone who wants to go into this old history can forget about Tartars and Montenegrins. It's best to start with the Finns. The book on the Michigan mining area was polite. It said the Finns were independent spirits who left the mines because they preferred homesteading. The Minnesota book was more to the point. It said they were fired and banned from the mines. That's the price they paid for being early organizers of the workforce. But that only brings up another problem with these ethnic studies. Unless you stick with cooking and handicrafts, you find yourself in the middle of Midwestern history.

The people on the land, the ones who were growing the crops and mining the ores, were the new American settlers in the new American states. There were places, Gopher Prairie for example, where it helped to be "possessed of grandparents born in America." Other places, Hibbing for example, had more sensible concerns—money and jobs. The fact is that the old timers organized as Midwestern Americans, and took on the eastern mine owners.

The big hole's in Hibbing because Hibbing incorporated to include the big hole. That way they could tax the mine owners. The town had the good sense to do a first class job of taking care of itself, and the money was spent on good living. Maybe it's a reaction to mines being ugly, but when mining towns get money they put a lot of emphasis on being pretty. I've noticed that before in parts of Pennsylvania. And it's something that really comes out in Hibbing. Nothing gaudy, just pretty—pleasant surroundings after a hard day in the mine. And the only place where they differed from other parts of America is that they could afford to be a little ahead of the rest of us in electrification, good civic buildings, and education. The only thing I can figure on Sinclair Lewis is that he didn't visit here before writing those lines about a teacher. Vida Sherwin would never have left the old Hibbing school system, and she would have loved the town.

Racing back to Route 2 lodgings on that earlier trip was a bad decision. The town's a delight, and you can still see the effects of some of the old free spending tax revenue days. Downtown's bright and cheery. Residential areas are well kept. The junior college is impressive. The Paulucci Planetarium is fascinating. And, unless you drive right up to the edge of it, you harly even notice the big hole in the ground. But it's there.

How do you explain that kind of a hole? They started digging and they didn't know when to stop. They even relocated part of the town, back in 1918, because it was in the way of the hole. The digging went on. They moved in all sorts of heavy equipment, even built a railroad down the side of it so they could keep on out loading the ore. Hundreds and hundreds of millions of tons were moved out. The Department of the Interior came around in 1966 and, not knowing anything else to do, they said it was an historic monument, the world's largest man-made hole in the ground. Since then something else has come along to be a bigger excavation, and they'll be still others making new records. But don't let that bother you. This is the original, the granddaddy of all big holes in the ground. Loking down, I'd guess it's also the Country's ugliest historic monument. It's miles around, all dirt, ragged features, and it looks like there's a muddy lake forming on the bottom. Anyone finding themselves down there would have to be either a mountain climber or a billy goat to get out. And, as usual, so long as they're stupendous, we're fascinated by ugly things.

But I don't want to leave on an ugly note. That wouldn't be honest. And I most certainly don't want to leave anyone with the impression that the ores are played out. Thanks to modern technology, there's many years supply left on this grand range. And that brings up my final surprise on this little side trip, the grandeur of the setting—something, I'm happy to say, Terry saw and enjoyed too. It's shield, and the ores go back to pre-Cambrian times. But it's a different development, a different face of the shield. It's wide open terrain with the range, various long hills, rising sharply for hundreds of feet from a flat plain. It's different, big open country with long views and rising breaks on the horizon. The overall effect is startling, but ruggedly appealing. It's been a good side trip.

History

Just a few words on how this State happened to become a part of the United States. This was part of the Louisiana Territory. At the time, administratively speaking, it was a Spanish territory, although the small white population was still mostly French. Property wise, a treaty had been signed in Europe and the territory was being returned to French ownership. It was just legal niceties, another hollow land title, so much paperwork. Napoleon had toyed with the idea of an overseas empire, but things didn't work out, and he had sense enough to know, paper titles notwithstanding, they wouldn't work out. Everyone was preparing for another European war. Even if he could spare the troops, he had no safe way to transport and maintain them in America.

On top of everything else, Napoleon found out that French rule over the Louisiana Territory was not acceptable to the United States. Jefferson, in his own subtle way, did a brilliant job of getting the message across. We would like to have the French as friends, but not as neighbors. We didn't want them in charge of Mississippi River navigation, and we didn't want them back in the Indian territories. The old frontier emotions were still strong and, as always, the Indians could be expected to flock to the beloved French standard. That record is amazing. To this day, local Indian historians still write with nostalgia of the old French friendship. But America couldn't tolerate a resumption of that old alliance and, anyway, France wasn't in a position to support the territory. Napoleon, always a realist, decided to sell the piece of paper, get cash for the war, and keep America's friendship. And did it ever work to our advantage. If you think about it you really can feel part of it when you spend some time around Lake Itasca and consider all that the Mississippi River means to America.

Lake Itasca

Minnesota moved in time. The land around Lake Itasca was turned into a state park before the lumber companies finished cutting through the whole areaa. Everyone's on their own, incidentally, in rating what was saved. The state has fenced in the tallest white pine tree in Minnesota—131 feet. The old British Navy specifications had a minimum acceptable length for white pine masts—112 feet. After a couple of hundred years of cutting, we have to come all the way out here to find one that meets the old specs. God save the Queen and hooray for the great State of Minnesota.

I finally found the tall white pines and they look just fine. I'm not sure, though, any of us would want them dominating our eastern countryside again. We've tailored everything to our tastes, needs, and fears of what might fall on the house, and it's hard to imagine trees this size all over the landscape. They're no longer part of our environment, and there just doesn't seem to be room for two hundred year old native pine trees. But at least they still belong in this park.

This is how America used to be, hidden lakes, free flowing streams, cool forests, and tall trees. It's laid out for visitor traffic, but these are the same trees that Schoolcraft saw. The Mississippi still comes from its original native American surroundings. It's only another small, what Lt. Allen called a "respectable stream," but there's a thrill in being in these surroundings and watching it come out of the lake. There's a nice touch, too, in having a wooden plank bridge, and a set of rocks, so tourists can walk across the Mississippi. Me? I did both. I walked across the bridge and came back across the rocks.

After a while, though, I did find a quiet place, off a little by itself, where I could sit and daydream. I dropped a twig into the water, watched it drift off, and wondered how long before it would float past New Orleans. Most likely it will never get there, it will be caught into a bank and reabsorbed into its native soil. Maybe it will get there, though, in a few months or, in whatever form, in a few centuries. It will float along north and east through swamps, lakes, and woodlands as the river seeks its southern route. It will float on a looped course through Minnesota's twin cities, traveling as much east as south until it leaves its native state, and then it will head straight south. It's at this point that the river becomes the great dividing line of the country. As the little twig speeds along, they'll be different states on each bank. The east will be on the left, the west on the right, and the trip will be glorious. It will float past Dubuque, Mark Twain's Hannibal, St. Louis and Memphis as the waters of the Missouri, Ohio, Arkansas, Red, and other great and small rivers join in to make a mighty surge past New Orleans as this greatest of all North American rivers completes its 2552 mile journey to the Gulf of Mexico.

The twig went off with my best wishes and fond memories. It was then, off to myself, that I started thinking back and daydreaming of the best family vacation we ever had. That was back in the years when I was lucky to get two weeks at a time, the kids were in their teens, and Terry was scrimping and saving so we could afford one good trip. It was our big family adventure and we wanted everything to go right. We got some travel brochures, explained our limits, and let the kids join in on the vote on where we should go. The vote was unanimous. Everyone wanted to go to Texas.

Our oldest daughter, Mary-Ellen, usually took charge of the logisitcs for those trips and she was good. Now she's a member of some professional society of logisticians and I still think she learned that part of her trade on family vacations. The eight of us traveled in the old station wagon, one with the luggage in the rear deck, four in the back seat, and three in front. With motel ice for refrigeration, we kept a supply of milk, bread, peanut butter, jelly, donuts, and those small individual boxes of packaged breakfast cereal, the kind that permit you to cut along the dotted lines and fold back the flaps so you can pour milk into the box. Breakfast was cereal and donuts, lunch was sandwiches, and dinner was either a fast food restaurant or a cafeteria.

We used to start travel days at four a.m. so we could have an early arrival at some city en route and, more often than not, it was the kids who were up first and knocking on our door. It was their vacation. They were always ready for the next adventure and, at that age, they had opinions and tastes. The one afternoon in New Orleans Latin Quarter was worth all the early rising. Tastes, and definitions of grace and charm, were broadened. Everyone explored and found things to admire, and we all shared in the thrill of discovery. There were balconies, railings, the lines, shapes and colors of buildings, courtyards, squares, sidewalk art displays, the old cathedral, the market, and, of course, the other end of the Mississippi River. Even if Texas didn't work out, the vacation was a success.

But Texas did work out. We spent a week in a lakefront cottage in those beautiful hills west of Austin, and it was a perfect first introduction to the west. On the lazy days we enjoyed swimming, boating, and meeting friendly Texans. On other days we made trips to San Antonio and Ciudad Acuna, Mexico. We saw buzzards on the branches of a dead tree, caught and released lizards, and marveled at the differences in vegetation and scenery. With everyone buying souvenirs, the wagon was more crowded than ever on the return trip. But there were no complaints. It was a happy vacation.

Bon voyage twig. Give my regards to the gulf states. And, while you're at it, remind them of your beautiful native forest homeland.

NORTH DAKOTA

Grand Forks

Someone lost a prairie, a great big historic open prairie. Not me. As usual, I take no responsibility for whatever I happen to find while traveling or reading. It was a lot of other people who lost it. Start with the folks at the University of North Dakota. Tree planting's been their big thing all through the years. Look at their old promotional books and you'll find hundred plus years old turn of the century type photographs, pretty co-eds with long modest dresses smiling up from the middle of a dirty mud hole. They've just done their annual thing. They've planted another tree. I think it had something to do with bringing civilization to the prairie.

So now people drive through Grand Forks, North Dakota without finding the prairie. After Crookston, Minnesota I started seeing more fields, and the grass looked a little different, a little more yellowish. That probably has more to do with the time of the year. A State of Minnesota sign lets everybody know when they enter the Red River Valley, and it does a nice job of pointing out some ancient high water boundaries. The valley used to be submerged under one long arm of a gigantic glacial lake that reached down from the Canadian plains. At another point there was a big rainbow stretching across the sky. All in all it was a pleasant drive, good poking around country, neat little towns, lots of trees, and rich farms—but the prairie's gone.

This, of course, is just initial surprise, not a complaint. The prairie can wait. The country-side, Grand Forks, and the University look wonderful just as they are, and the trees really do belong. Geographers draw lines down the map and explain why there's limited woody growth west of one line where the annual rainfall is less than twenty inches, and less again where the annual rainfall is less than fourteen or seventeen inches or something. Then they throw in temperatures, seasonal variations, altitude figures, and evaporation rates, and it gets progressively drier and more barren as you travel toward the Rocky Mountains. But these lines and conditions are all west of Grand Forks. As it turns out, nobody seems to know why the treeless prairie was all the way from here to Crookston in the first place. There's some speculation about Indians burning trees, buffalo herds trampling them, and things like that. Maybe it was a forest that was lost way back when, and I was just looking for the wrong thing.

I did better this time around when I spent time in The Greenway, the park area on both sides of the River, and followed the path to town. The river forks are pleasant and peaceful. I threw twigs in the Red River of the North and got a kick out of knowing that, in just a couple of days, I've sent little messages to both ends of the continent. This river flows north, and the twigs are off on a long indirect journey to Hudson Bay. Another message? Sure, why not? Tell them everyone here did a beautiful job of keeping the river banks in a nice natural state. Oh, and while you're at it, ask them to hold a seat for me on the Polar Bear Express. I'm still dreaming of getting back there. But that's for later. For now I'm still in The Greenway, and I've found a link with the past.

There's a newer railroad bridge, supported all the way across the river by sturdy stone pillars. Then the tracks continue on an old wooden trestle bridge which still looks solid and sturdy. From the looks of it, I'd guess it dates back to the "Dakota fever" years of the 1880s, the time when thousands of families came from the east and Europe, especially Scandinavia, to fill up the Dakota prairies. There's a story here, or a lot of stories, but I'm not the story teller.

History is grand sweep and official record. It tells us how many people came, and over what period of time. It tells us about shenanigans in territorial seats of government, the comings and goings, schemes, thefts, and power plays of politicians, speculators, and railroad tycoons. It's interesting. But none of this gives any insight into the feelings and thoughts, hopes, dreams, and lives of these people.

It wasn't an organized group coming under a charter like the Puritans in Massachusetts, or the Quakers in Pennsylvania. It wasn't the old frontier creeping ahead a mile at a time, weaving its way through established wagon trails. This was a new frontier, millions of square miles of land, wide open, new, cleared of hostile Indians, and ready for immediate settlement. Maybe the people came because they knew this was the end of the frontier, the last unused space in the United States.

It was people, individuals and families. They bundled up whatever few goods they had and came from Norway, Germany, Canada, New England, Maryland, the old South, and all points in between, people out for a new start in life. And the prairies and plains kept filling up with families, people who came quietly, kept few records, and filled the land. So there you have it. I think Jim Hill's railroad took them across the wooden trestle, and I don't know how to follow the story after that. So let's get on to a more recent story.

The flood of the century, as it was called at the time, has elements of disaster, courage, and determination. It was only back in 1997 and most of us remember the horror of watching on television as things went from bad to worse. Winter had been brutal and there was a tremendous snow pack. The melt came too fast and the flood was irresistible and high on both sides of the river. The toll on animals, especially cattle, was especially harsh. The toll on humans was even more sad. Over fifty thousand people had to be evacuated; this was the largest civilian evacuation since the Civil War. And, to top it all off, a series of fires added to the flood damage.

The Route 2 visitor's center has a short video that gives good coverage to all this, and it even has some literature on the rebuilding. But there's nothing that can do full justice to that. It's incredible. Only nine years after that disaster and the cities, on both sides of the river, look as if nothing ever happened here. They just look like a couple of clean, well kept cities with some new and restored buildings

This, I should point out, is both introduction to—and definition of—the State of North Dakota. The people work with skill and determination; projects are well organized; and attitudes are positive.

Fort Totten and Devils Lake

On February 27, 1876 Private Vetter wrote to his brother in Pittsburgh. It is a normal family letter, talk of weather, the boredom of garrison duty in isolated Fort Totten, and the cost of clothing. Apparently their mother was still in Germany. There was some concern for her health, and a hope that she would write soon. In the meantime the brother was not to send any more letters until he got a new address. Private Michael Vetter was being assigned to General Custer's command.

It's sad, terribly sad to read that letter. Rest Private Vetter, rest in peace. Your letters are preserved and on display along with other honored military mementos. You're not forgotten. People still read them and pause for a silent moment. I'll get back to the fort in a little while but, for now, with respect, I'm going to move on to Devils Lake.

Captain E. E. Herman built a steamboat and called it the "Minnie H" after his daughter. It must have been a pretty good boat. He sailed it around Devils Lake for twenty-four years, through until 1907. He made the rounds carrying freight, mail, and passengers between the city of Devils Lake, Minnewaukan, and Fort Totten. And, at the end, it wasn't the boat that gave out, it was the lake. It receded and shrank to the point where it became too shallow for a steamboat.

Now there's a grammar school named "Minnie H" in the city of Devils Lake. It's a modern type school, long, low, cheerful colors, and lots of window space. It's in a pleasant settled neighborhood. On a straight line from the school, down Walnut Street, you have a law enforcement center, an insurance company office, a small office building, a human services center, a service road, Route 2, a sandwich shop, a very large field, then Route 20 and, if you follow that for a mile or so, you will get to Devils Lake. That's how far the lake has receded since Captain Herman's time. It used to be all the way to where the school is now. As a matter of fact, that's where he used to dock his boat.

I don't know the measurements. The WPA book, which was written in the 1930s, says the lake receded four miles from the city of Devils Lake, six miles from Minnewaukan, and about two and a half miles from Fort Totten. But this is all past and, until recently, the explanations were along these lines: The Rocky Mountains went through an upheaval and rose to something like their present height about five million years ago. The clouds were blocked. Less rain could get through from the west. Now geographers draw those lines on maps. This place is west of the 98th meridian, which means less than twenty inches of rain per year. Geography, as well as history, points to the drying up of Devils Lake.

What actually happened? So far, the reverse. The low point was around 1940. After that the lake settled down and even started to grow some. Then, in 1993, there was some kind of a local weather change with greatly increased rain and snow. It's serious, to the point where the lake reclaimed thousands of acres of land and levees had to be built to contain the water. Now the fear is that, if the levees break, the water will come all the way up to the Minnie H School. And the scientists think there's a good possibility of several more years of increased rain. But don't worry. You can bet on North Dakota to keep things under control. They've got a nice state, and they're going to keep it that way.

That's my real point, of course, not the rain level or the extent to which the lake is down or up, but that the whole area is so nice to see. More or less arid only means different varieties of scenery. It has nothing to do with attractiveness. Besides, I'm still in the eastern part of North Dakota and, despite sometimes low rainfall, the area doesn't look arid. It's prairie. That started just after Grand Forks, gently rolling prairie with few trees, and mile after mile of dark brown farmland. But the land is lush and there are some features that don't belong in a prairie setting.

The steamboat isn't coming back, but the lake is still here, miles and miles of it, light blue and translucent. It's a popular place with vacationers hunters, fishermen, and a host of small boat owners. And that awful name only refers to some old Indian Spirits who were angry because of the way the Chippewa and the Sioux tribes were fighting over the property. One dark night both tribes sent braves out in canoes on a sneak raiding party. A storm came, capsized the canoes, and the braves drowned. The Indians said the place was governed by angry spirits. The settlers, hearing this, called it Devils Lake.

We can't blame the spirits for being angry. They provided rich brown prairie, a lake big enough for steamboat travel, some hills, and a nice big hardwood forest. What they got back was fighting and breaking of taboos. But that's all old business—other days, other wars. Things are peaceful here now, and the spirits seem to be smiling.

The hills and trees are in the Fort Totten area, and that's another oddity in this prairie setting. Odd, out of place, but very nice forest, even when you're driving around in it. And the fort fits in like a natural part of the scenery. Maybe it looks so comfortable and in place because it never did anything to upset the spirits—no wars, no battles, just a well preserved frontier post. The guide says this disturbs some of the young visitors. They want blood. Sorry kids. But if you walk around and check out a few things, you'll get a good understanding of garrison duty. And ask the guide some questions. She's smart, very friendly, and she has some good stories. Just stop looking for blood. The old spirits already punished a couple of other tribes for that kind of behavior.

The West Begins

There's land, wide open land and weather. Nothing else, or at least nothing else that counts for much. The land rolls on—hundreds of miles across, and thousands of miles up and down. The weather keeps playing across the surface and doing strange things, howling, freezing, baking, smiling, and blowing, always blowing. These are the main actors. Everything and everyone else has bit parts, on stage for a few years, or a few hundred years. They're nice little parts and interesting to see, but they're not the main show,

For example, there are hundreds of millions of trees out here. You'd never guess it driving along, especially as you drive further west. But it's so. President Franklin Roosevelt had well over two hundred million trees planted in the 1930s when he was trying to stop some terrible blowing dust storms. You can still see many of these shelterbelts, long rows of trees here and there across the prairie. Trees grow naturally alongside of rivers and in a few isolated forest areas, places like the badlands and the hills around Fort Totten. They're here, too, wherever man cares enough to keep his old friends around. You see them in cities and towns, and you see them, close packed and three or four rows deep, all around isolated farm houses. They're planted to surround the house like a high tapered hedge. It's for protection, shade in summer, and a buffer against snow and wind in winter. But, overall, the land is so immense that these few hundred million trees seem insignificant. And it's not just the trees.

Minot's another example. It's a nice city, typical North Dakota, clean, pleasant, friendly people, and good solid construction. I wouldn't be at all surprised if it turns out to be one of the things that stays around for a few hundred years. But it will never really belong. It will always look like what it is, a city that's been forced on the land. It's no less a city for that, maybe more. The people certainly seem to think they're better off. They even think they're getting extra benefits from a majestically indifferent environment. But that's typical too. It's the kind of thing they're always believing in North Dakota.

The State started with boosterism, and I can't see where anything's changed. It's some kind of an ingrained thing that goes with the territory. At first it was all those boasts about quick riches, and how this is a healthier place to live. Now they crank out handouts on farm wealth, and about how North Dakota factory workers are more productive than other factory workers. And it doesn't do any good to question any of these claims. Someone from the State capitol or the university will produce convincing figures to "prove" that it's true. But I never know whether it was true to start with, or whether they started with a brag and then did a lot of work to make it come true. It's like the old better health claims. To hear the claims, you'd believe something in the air gave good health. Apparently something worked. Teddy Roosevelt came out here a sick and dispirited young man, recovered completely, and later led the Rough Riders on a charge up San Juan Hill. And the present day people certainly do look vigorous and healthy. But both Grand Forks and Minot have first rate hospital complexes to keep them that way. Regardless, North Dakota will go on giving credit to something in the air and, if pressed, they'll probably prove something.

Until then, though, I'm not going along with any claims about this clean air. If there's anything about the good health business, I think it probably has something to do with the people themselves, and their reasons for choosing to live here. The land's big. Human nature counts for more. People are more likely to believe their individual actions make a difference—the Sioux decoy dressed in buffalo skins on a tribal hunt; Teddy Roosevelt on a round-up; Ole Rolvaag competing to be the best on a team at pitching grain; a homestead wife spending precious time and water on a flower garden; and the helpful young lady in the Williston Chamber of Commerce. She combines enthusiasm with personality and it's infectious. They've been this way all along. They believe in themselves. Maybe this explains something about health, flood restoration, factory productivity, and farm wealth.

U. S. ROUTE 2 - CANADA TOO!

Still and all though, it remains to be seen if even the farmers are going to make any permanent changes out here. They deserve credit because they're good at what they do, big engineering projects, careful land management, and tremendous harvests. Food for America and the world. Very impressive, but it may only be surface changes. There doesn't seem to be much change in the basic character of the land. Cut off the water supply and it will go right back to playing dusty games with the wind. As a matter of fact, I did see some swirls, not many, and not very big, just a few incidental reminders of an underlying natural order. But, at least for now, it's the dust that looks unnatural and out of place in this rich farmland.

So let's get away from land management and other such serious matters. This place has cows and ducks. They're fun to watch, especially the ducks. The land's dotted with hundreds of little artificial ponds, water holes for livestock, and irrigation run-off puddles. The cows are interesting, usually just standing around and munching, sometimes walking, a few times running, once in a while you see one in the water and, when you get tired of watching them, you can still go on watching those more interesting critters—the ducks. There is something everlastingly endearing about wild ducks, and there are thousands of them along this route. When you watch them in small groups, sometimes only two in a pond, they're especially fascinating. They're such busy little creatures, paddling around, bobbing up and down, and splashing their wings. They're also fit and sleek, just about ready for a trip south. No hurry though. They'll stay as long as they can. They know a good thing when they see it.

The setting's earthy rich and autumn warm. It's a place for artists as well as ducks, but they'd have to be very good artists. Never mind the usual rules of composition. No houses or trees standing off center. They're not the story. And no reliance on shading or shadows. Open rolling space all the way to the horizon. Clear air, bright sunshine, and robust colors. Big blue sky and small blue ponds. Brown earth, different shades of brown and sometimes, when it's freshly turned, black. Green fields, yellow flowers, gold stubble, and rolled hay. Wheat, a lighter shade of gold, and sunflowers with their deep brown faces folded over and facing east. In fairness, though, let me also offer a tip for artists who need buildings. Go to Denbigh and paint a picture of the big old empty building, I think it was a schoolhouse, with the purple roof. Capture the spirit of that building and your fame's assured. Meanwhile, I'm going to go on doing what I've been doing. Enjoying the country.

The sun's shining, the ducks are paddling, Artemus is purring along, and I have nothing better to do than enjoy the sights and sounds—nature's big stage and man's little additions. There's always something to see. Rugby has an oblisk on a cement platform with Mexican, Canadian, and American flags flying behind it. It's a fun place to stop, eat, clown, and take some pictures. It's the geographic center of the North American continent. At one point, in driving along, I found myself measuring a passing fright train. I figured it was something over a mile and a quarter. Prairie freight trains actually look romantic, especially at a distance. They look brave, small, and important—Jim Hill's vision, the settlers lifeline. And I hear their long whistles at night. People say it's a lonely sound across the prairie. I think it's thrilling.

I spent a day in Minot and two days taking trips from Williston. The cities, of course, have all the modern conveniences, amenities, and comforts. I'm enjoying it all but, at least while still in town, I spend more time looking for what's left over from early settler days. It's here, it's in people's friendly, open attitudes, the layout of some of the older stores, and the look of the churches. Ole Rolvaag believed pastors were more humble and human in America, and that the church, more than any other institution, saved the immigrants from going to the dogs. It's probably some of this background that gives Minot's downtown Lutheran Church such a gentle and inviting appearance. Still, for all the nice things, there's still only one overwhelming impression out here—the land. There's so much of it, and I can't seem to get enough of it.

A telling story can be seen in some swirls on N. Broadway, just up the hill from Minot State University. But the major show of swirls is in the hills west of Minot. Nature doesn't hide its past in this wide open land. It flaunts it. We read about glaciers and great swirling floods that shaped the land. Then you come to the swirled hills of Minot and the picture's complete. All that's left now, in the wake of the great floods, is the Souris River, a pleasant little river meandering along the valley and through the city. But, just in riding along this section of Route 2, you can see and marvel at the swirls in the sides of the hills. It doesn't take much imagination to picture the might and force of what happened here.

Something that turned out to be a lot of fun, incidentally, was taking back roads and getting lost. I did that between Minot and Williston when I was chasing down the location of an original Route 2, and some old railroad history. The reasons don't matter. The fun is driving along for mile after mile in this rich varied land, and being the only one on the road. In fact, even on Route 2, this is the emptiest stretch of road I've seen, but I don't feel lonesome. It's the great plains now, no longer the prairie. The change came when I drove up the hill outside of Minot. But that, again, is a geographer's distinction. It looks like the same rich land with the same entertaining ducks, and about the only different thing for me is that I feel carefree. And, of course, I never really felt lost. It's just that sometimes it takes me longer than I figured to work my way back to Route 2.

But the carefree feeling is something that surprised me. Ever since I started going through this big country I've been feeling light hearted and carefree, and I don't know why. I expected it would be lonesome, or at least tiresome. Not so. I'm fascinated. The land's always interesting and frequently awesome—and here I'm talking about the White Earth River area. It's wide open empty country with tremendous moulded shapes—contours, hills, and ravines, the old west of everyone's dreams. Here, if anywhere, I might have felt lonesome, but I didn't. I just kept driving around, admiring, and enjoying. I feel great. It must be something in the food. I'd hate to have anyone think I'm the type who could be taken in by all that old boosterism talk about the air being healthier. Besides, it's time to get around to my side trips and, for a change, this brings me to a scary place

The Badlands

I spent an afternoon poking around the northern part of the Badlands by way of paying my respects to Theodore Roosevelt, a man who, after all these years, still strikes me as the most forceful character in American history. Always testing himself, testing rules, pushing for the limits, trying everything and everybody to see how far he could exert his own will. His high toned friend, Henry Adams, once wrote, "Power when wielded by abnormal energy is the most serious of facts, and Roosevelt's friends knew that his restless and combative energy was more than abnormal." Although it doesn't cover his intelligence and patriotism, that was undoubtedly a fair description of his restless personality. He was a restless man who had an abnormal amount of combative energy, even to the point of making his friends nervous. No matter what he was doing, he always looked for a way, the most extreme way he could find, to make it a challenge.

I expect that's why he loved the Badlands as much as he did. It was one of the wildest challenges he ever found, an early testing ground for his incredible energy and combativeness. And all stories are true. He actually lived the life of a cowboy while he was here. He faced down gunmen, chased and captured desperadoes, and raced horses across the country at breakneck speed so he could head off, and round up, unruly cows. Bully for you Mr. President, and respects from a timid soul who could never qualify as a rough rider. I wouldn't take a four wheel drive truck across this country at more than ten miles an hour. But I think your range choice more than lives up to the reputation you gave it. It's unpredictable, weird, grotesque, fantastic, and contorted in every way that glacial floods could work on sandstone. Now the whole area is set aside as the Theodore Roosevelt National Park, a worthy memorial to your courageous spirit. And there's a good fourteen mile road with overlooks and helpful signs for visitors like me. Another good side trip. Now on to the next one.

Fort Union and Fort Buford

Looks like Fort Union is going to get the lion's share of the trade again. The other fort, Fort Buford, is a few miles down a side road, off to itself dreaming old dreams with empty rivers, mud flats and graves. Fort Union is right on North Dakota Highway 1804, and the Depatment of the Interior is turning this site into a showplace of early American history.

This is an obvious place for a fort. It's near where the Missouri and the Yellowstone Rivers come together. Lewis and Clark took one look at this juncture, or confluence as they call it out here, and started discussing the siting for a fort. But they were thinking of a military fort and that's not what happened—or at least it didn't happen until a long time later. What happened is that fur traders moved in. As usual, they were out in advance of the frontier, and pretty much beyond the rule of law. They would set up shop in Indian country, and live by their own rules. There were some bad parts. Any halfway complete history of the period and the trade will devote large sections to describing some grubby attitudes and brutal competitive practices. There were good things too. The better traders had business ability and imagination, and they were providing necessary goods to Indian customers. Fort Union is a good place to learn about these things. The old trade never saw a tougher competitor, or a more successful and flamboyant winner than Kenneth McKenzie, the builder and resident manager of Fort Union.

There are teepees off to one side. The archeologists have done a thorough job of rebuilding the walls and spotting some other building locations. Most of all, though, they deserve credit for a reconstruction of McKenzie's great house. The man lived and entertained like a king. Almost two thousand miles upstream from St. Louis, and he was hosting formal parties for visiting artists, rich adventurers, and European noblemen. Dress at the head table was formal, the cuisine was first class, and the meal was sometimes followed by a dance. And the dance partners were pretty young Indian women dressed like fashion models. This part wasn't discussed by the guide. Just as well. There were children in the audience. Anyway, the social life was just the style, not the substance of the fort.

Fort Union lasted for thirty-eight years. It stood for some kind of rough equality with the Indians, bargaining equality that is, not trust. There was a double set of gates on the fort. Indians were allowed inside the first gate, into a trading area. They were not allowed through the second gate, into the fort proper. The frontier never forgot the lesson of

Fort Michilmackinac. So, except for a few kept girls, Indians weren't invited to McKenzie's parties. Then too, McKenzie wasn't sending soldiers, miners, or settlers out to invade the plains. He was just a fur trader, someone who exchanged manufactured goods for furs. It was the old familiar trade. Indians could tolerate it.

The Sioux attacked in 1860. They were repulsed, but Fort Union's days were coming to an end. McKenzie was long gone, the fur trade was declining, and the Indians were no longer tolerant. Too many steamboats on the Missouri River; too many whites invading the plains. The attempt to stop the process was ferocious but futile. As Fort Union was being torn down, the most hated of all places, Fort Buford, was being built right down at the confluence of the rivers. The United States Army was showing its power in land claimed by the Sioux. It was the beginning of the end.

This was just about the center of the last Indian area, the final frontier of American history. The poorly defined treaty lands, the land west of the Missouri River, the high plains areas of the Dakotas, Wyoming, and Montana, were still home to wandering bands of Indians. But the army had moved in and, unless the process was stopped, the settlers would follow. There were settled states and territories to the east and south. The west, from the Pacific coast through to the end of the Rocky Mountains, was already filling up with miners, lumber men, homesteaders, and towns. Only the least wanted land, the trackless northern area of the Great American Desert, was still in dispute between Indians and whites.

A lot has been written and filmed about the final takeover of these plaims areas from the Indians. Some of it almost makes it look like a contest. It wasn't. There were Indian raids, and there was some fighting. Red Cloud and his warriors succeeded in closing the Bozeman Trail. General Sully had a bad time of it when he forced a march through the badlands. General Custer was caught where he shouldn't have been. But there was never really any contest, not in the sense of there being any doubt about the outcome. Civilization was moving in. The process was inexorable.

Honor the Sioux. Their love of homeland was fierce, and their spirit was bold. Still, their cause was lost. They couldn't close Fort Buford. Sitting Bull and his braves attacked boats along the river. All land movements to and from the fort were subject to surprise attack.

This went on for years. Downstream, back in the States as the local expression went, the rumor spread one year that Fort Buford had fallen during the winter. It hadn't. For all their rage, the Indians couldn't take a fort. Buford stayed. The Army prevailed. Crazy Horse was killed. Sitting Bull languished in Canadian exile. And the last free Indians in America were moved on to reservations. Later, Sitting Bull would return and be directed to surrender at Fort Buford. Cruel fate. The cemetery's well kept. There's a white picket fence around it. The gravestones list the names and causes of death—disease, inebriation, or killed by Indians. And there's an interpretive center just down the street with a good overlook of the confluence. I was the only visitor, and I spent a couple of hours just wandering around. It's amazing how out of the way, peaceful, and relaxing the setting is. There are a couple of old fort buildings left. Along with the military mementoes, there are some old river maps, and the lady in charge does a nice job of pointing out the changes. There are big open fields. There's a park where you can sit and watch the rivers flow into each other. They're wide, clean, and empty now. There are sand spits, fairly wide mud caked flats, a good water flow, and nice trees. It's almost back to the way it must have looked when Lewis and Clark came through.

MONTANA

Beauty, Promise—and Harsh Reality

At about mid-morning, driving through the Fort Peck Indian Reservation, I saw six would be wild horses trotting along on the opposite side of the road. Not wild, just would be wild. They were obviously ranch horses that had escaped through a fence somewhere. Whatever open area they might have on the reservation side, they were out of place on the highway side of the fence. I stopped to watch and take a picture but my interest was resented. They gave me challenging looks, so much as to say, "Stay on your own side of the road." That's what the looks meant. I've never read any studies on horse manners and mentality, but it was obvious. They were warning me. They had broken loose, and I was not to interfere. I turned around and followed, but only for a couple of minutes. I was afraid of making them nervous. Then I settled for parking on the side of the road and watching until they were out of sight. They looked so brave and proud trotting free on the side of Route 2.

They won't make it. Some angry owner in a pickup truck will catch up with them sooner or later, and that will be the end of freedom. Too bad. As usual in Montana there were hills in the distance and I kept thinking that, if only they could turn in that direction, and make it to the hills, they might stay free. But there were fences along both sides of the road. Even if they knew the difference, they couldn't turn. They'll be caught and returned to their own pasture.

Tough luck horses, but don't take it too hard. You're probably only being saved from your own folly. And, yes, I have some understanding

U. S. ROUTE 2 - CANADA TOO!

of the attraction. The land's full of enticement and promise, horizon after horizon, with open, soft brown and gold rolling plains. It says come, live and be free in the great open space of America. It entices with beauty and the feel of freedom. But it's not to be trusted. It misleads and deceives. It pleases and lulls, then it turns on people and animals with every terrible weapon known to nature.

Nature's rules for the use of the land are easy enough to understand. If land grows grass, it is grazing land, a place that can feed cows and sheep. If it grows crops—wheat, corn, vegetables, or fruit—it is farmland, a place that can feed people. If it can not grow grass or crops, it is unproductive. If it can grow grass or crops sometimes, but not other times, it is unreliable.

These northern plains are unreliable grazing land. Sometimes the herds do well. Sometimes they die in winter. As farmland, the area is unproductive in some places, and unreliable in others. Parts of it just won't grow crops. Other parts grow crops but fail periodically because of drought.

The story out here is all about how people learned these lessons. Local history books read like catalogs of years. There are good years, the years that entice people in to build and invest. Next there are bad years, the years that destroy the investments. Then there's another cycle of good years. The land sits in shining beauty and entices the next set of victims.

The winter of 1886-87 is still legendary in the cattle business. It was boom time on the high plains. European and American interests, smart money investors, empire builders, Teddy Roosevelt and other owner-operators—they were all over the plains with growing herds of cattle. Experience had shown there wouldn't be more than a ten percent winter loss and, in those years, that was tolerable. Then nature showed one full season of howling artic power. It was death for the cattle and ruination for the owners. I won't recite the details. They're gruesome. Anyone who wants an ugly picture of what happened can look at the starving steer picture in a Charlie Russell art book; it's usually entitled "Last of 5,000." The ranching business came back, at least for a while, but a lot of the old owners didn't. Even Teddy Roosevelt lost heart. He kept the property for a few years but he never went back to ranching.

There are more than enough cycles and victims. The ones I feel sorriest for are the thousands of farm families who came out here because they believed Jim Hill. You can still see some of their abandoned houses, small simple one story places with crumpling roofs and broken walls. The end of a dream. To be fair, though, Jim Hill didn't lie to them. He should have known better, but he believed his own hired experts and press releases.

All dreams ended, after four years of drought, with the terrible winter of 1920-21. It was all shortly after Jim Hill died. Amazing man. Amazing life. So long as he was around and running things, nature behaved. It went into one of its wet cycles when he started the promotion and, for so long as he lived, the rains came and the plains had good crops. And, for the most part, his victims didn't turn against him either. Why blame his memory? Even in the midst of disaster, why blame the memory of a man who sincerely believed in family farming and American know how? It wasn't Jim's fault that the rains stopped, the crops wasted, and the naked earth blew away.

In Joe Howard's popular book on this story, it was the heartless eastern financial interests, the cruel Federal Reserve System above all, that caused so much of the suffering that went along with the abandonment of the family farms. But they only added to the misery, they didn't cause the catastrophe. Nature ruled out family farming on these northern plains. One by one, the beaten families gave up the dream of having their own place, forfeited the property, packed their meager belongings, and moved on. They were bruised and abused. So was the land.

Despite all this, it's still predominately farm area, all the way from the North Dakota border to the Rocky Mountains. When producing, these northern counties of Montana are one of the world's great wheat growing areas, and no one's going to give that up. The difference today, to believe so many modern writers, is that now we've got things under control. We've replaced family farms with large scale farming enterprises, and they have the resources and know-how to reduce losses in bad years, and go on producing in good years. Sounds reasonable. Time will tell. Meanwhile, the land has a well groomed dazzling allure.

Wolf Point and Fort Peck

"Nothing in art or aught else" deserves praise, says Walt Whitman, unless it exudes western prairie scent and the atmosphere of of the Missouri River. Makes sense to me Walt, especially the part about the river. The steamboats are gone, incidentally, and the river seems to be hiding. What? How do you hide the wide winding Missouri, the longest river in North America? Easy. Build good straight roads, and cars that cruise comfortably at sixty plus miles per hour. It's a pretty good arrangement. Those hurried people aren't concerned with the "art or aught else." There's no point in bothering them with a slow old river. And that leaves the river to technicians and romantics—the people who care.

Who let the technicians into this? There's no way to keep them out. They're here and that's all there is to it. They're professionals working for big organizations. They have to do all that statistical bragging about the details of dams, volumes, acre feet, and kilovolt amperes. It's the job. On the human side, though, most of them seem to be working romantics. They care. They really like the countryside and rivers. It takes people like this to keep things working and nice. You get a good example of their care and skill when you drive around on the big dam they have at Fort Peck.

It's not an irregation dam. They're further west, up on the Milk and Marias Rivers. Fort Peck has the dam that supplies electricity all the way from here to the Rocky Mountains. When it was first built, back in the 1930s, it was touted as the world's largest earth fill dam. Now they just talk about the amount of electricity it generates. It's a reliable supplier, a good solid professional dam. It's a nice job, too, of having a dam blend in with its natural surroundings. There are natural hills on either side. The dam is almost just another hill, a smooth graceful rise that connects the hills on either side of the valley. But you really don't get the full effect until you drive up and along the top. On one side the whole valley is filled with water, a crisp clear lake that's fairly close to the level of the road. On the other side you look down a long powerful incline to see the Missouri River resume its old wandering course. And all this in the middle of a wide open, and nearly empty, high plains area. It's exhilarating.

Nice dam. But can dams have the scent and atmosphere we started with? Probably not, but that's getting picky. We'll lose the sense of Whitman if we try to pin him down literally. The dam deserves to be admired for its muted strength and soaring grace. For the rest of what Walt Whitman was talking about, you can find it in Wolf Point. I was there earlier and it turned out to be a convenient place to find old river and friendly people.

It's just another high plains town. People used to cut wood down by the river and sell it to passing steamships. Then there was a cowboy period, but that didn't last long. Jim Hill built his railroad and it became a settler town. That's what still shows—the old settler virtues—solid downtown, well kept homes, churches, and a school—always a school. Here they've got a neat looking school that's low and round, the kids should be impressed with the priority. It's a good place to stop. There are different things to see, and the people are easy going and jolly.

The big burley fellows in the truck stop restaurant talked and joked with me. One of them thought the town was named Wolf Point because of the time, back in the 1800s, when they poisoned all the wolves, and then had a few hundred carcasses piled up all winter. He told me where to look for an historic marker on this. I told him I heard that explanation, too, but the WPA book says the town was named after a bluff that was a landmark for pilots on the old steamships. They liked that story, too, and they gave me directions for getting to a lookout point on the river.

On the way I had a whole football team riding in front of me on the back of an open truck. They were full of good natured confidence about some game that was coming up, and they kept yelling about how they were "Number One." I tooted the horn, waved a clenched fist with a thumb up, and yelled hooray and good luck. Then they waved back, and yelled cheers for me as their truck turned off in another direction. Nice kids. Hope they won.

Like I said at the beginning of this, the river is pretty well hidden so you need directions to find it. It is stay on Fifth Avenue until it becomes a dirt road. Follow the dirt road to an open field at the end, cross the field and you'll find yourself on a bluff overlooking the Missouri River. It is not easy to get to, but there is a rough path.

There was a light breeze and a warm sun. The field was rutted dirt and yellow grass. The bluff looked to be about sixty feet high. It's steep and pock marked with erosion. And, down at the bottom, the Missouri is flowing along in the old bed it carved out for itself at the edge of the last big glacier. It's wide, calm, and peaceful as it flows around a large bend. It's a relaxing sight. Just strolling along the bluff, all alone, and watching the river was a nice way to mull over Whitman's comments, and wind up a happy day.

U. S. ROUTE 2 -CANADA TOO!

Charlie Russell and Progress

You can see the purple sage, not everywhere, but patches of it along the side of the road and in the dry gully areas between the road and the beginning of a farm field. It's something left over from earlier times, the old days when there were no railroads, and sage, animals, cowboys, and Indians had the run of the land. Some people, Charlie Russell for one, liked it better that way.

Russell was typical of so many early westerners. He was a westerner by choice, a mid-westerner who managed to leave a respectable home at an early age. He spent his adult years bumming around and riding herd in Montana. He even moved in and lived with some Blackfeet Indians for a few months. He was as carefree as can be and didn't want much. He got along very well with hand-outs, old clothes, riding herd, other occasional odd jobs, and drawing pictures for beer or grocery money. The only thing this happy go lucky cowboy ever needed was Montana.

Charlie wasn't bad. He was always good for a funny story. He was a little rowdy on occasion, and he liked the wild bunch, but he was too easy going and decent a fellow to be bad. It wasn't in him to do anything really harmful. He sure did seem to especially like some of those bad guys, however, but not just them. Actually he seemed to like everybody and everything in the west, good guys, bad guys, Indians, explorers, hunters, the animals they hunted, cowboys, and trail drivers. You can still see it in his paintings. And they were all so young—the whole west seemed so young and easy going. It doesn't matter whether sex, bank robbery, danger, violent death, or every day life was the subject, there's a refreshing innocence in Russell's matter of fact style. But that's getting ahead of the story.

So Charlie lived his early life the way he wanted, rode the range, sang to the cows, caroused with other cowboys, camped with Indians, and drew pictures for his friends. His well to do family back in Missouri couldn't understand it. They never understood him. His parents only let him come out here as a young fellow because they thought he'd stop dreaming of the nomad life of an adventurer once he was faced with the reality of the western wilderness. They thought he'd fail and return to the family business. But Charlie never wanted to be a businessman.

Another thing Charlie didn't want was to be an artist, at least not a commercial one. He probably earned his way with the Indian tribe by drawing pictures, and he used to draw pictures or make little clay statues for his friends or, as we have seen, for beer or grocery money. But that was fun. And everyone loved his pictures because they were so accurate, right down to the last detail. Charlie's mind worked that way. Once he saw a thing he'd remember it forever. Even when he was drawing or painting twenty years after the fact, the markings on the horse, the color and position of the bandana, even the amount of purple sage on the ground, was exactly right.

But he could no longer be a working cowboy. This stretch along Route 2 is the last area that Charlie Russell worked as a cowboy. He and others followed the great herds to these far northern ranges. Then Jim Hill pushed his railroad through and brought in all those farm families. Steel plows turned over the earth, buried the purple sage, and ended the open range.

Personally, I'm not upset with finding the purple sage pushed off to the gully. So far as I'm concerned the current land use is about the best we can do—the railroad, Route 2, towns, dams, and farmers growing wheat, hay, and sunflowers. None of the towns or cities are large. They're well spaced along the highway, settler sturdy, and, in many cases, they've managed to preserve some memory of the earlier cowboy background. Glasgow has a good shopping area and, if you're there at the right time, you can see cowboy skills at the state fair grounds. Chinook is where Charlie Russell lived when he was up here; it has tree shaded streets, a museum with displays of the time, before the Rocky Mountains began to rise, when Montana was a jungle area with strange prehistoric animals. Jim Hill's old rallying ground, Havre, is at the bottom of a hill and shows well, especially at night, when you come over the hill from the west. I'm taking the land as I find it, and I like what I see.

Like everyone else who has been enticed by this treacherous place, I think the land is spectacular. Everything in Montana is spectacular, land, sky, horizons, distant hills, and rivers. This is high plains country, dry, clear, open, and enticing. The towns and other modern improvements have opened it up, and they haven't done that much to change the essential character of this great land. But that's only my opinion. Westerners from earlier times, and some from recent times, would probably disagree.

For a long time now there's been a contrary streak in some of our more intelligent westerners. They understand, but fail to show proper respect for the progress of our civilization. Chet Huntly retired from TV to set up shop out here. A.B. Guthrie, Jr. wrote Montana novels in which characters could be honored, even though they knew their stand was futile, when they said no to progress. Mark Twain knew the comfort of railroad parlor cars and the luxury of first class steamship travel, but he went on insisting that the standard for delightful travel was a stagecoach ride he once had from Missouri to California. Charlie Russell fits in here too. He knew and ignored the work of the French artists of his own time; he kept his own vision, the unposed reality of the old west. But about the worst of this group would have to be the cowboy comedian, Will Rogers. He was another out of work cowboy and, before settling down to show business, he traveled all the way to Argentina trying to get a job as a working cowboy.

With that background it's no wonder Rogers and Russell wound up close friends. They were kindred spirits. They loved getting together to swap funny stories and Rogers, who bought several of the paintings, was a great admirer of Russell's art. But it was a kindred spirit from an earlier generation, Mark Twain, who came out with a working old west art principle that fits Russell's work.

On his Innocents Abroad trip, Twain kept looking at Europe's art treasures and squirming. He had good taste. He appreciated the beauty of most of what he saw; he accepted that the artists were "old masters;" he understood that their talents and techniques were admired by the ages, and he would have been happy to go along with the general consensus. But Twain had a problem. It was with the handling of the subject matter. Most of these artists did whatever was required to please their rich and powerful patrons. In one case Raphael pictured some "infernal villains—seated in heaven and conversing familiarly with the Virgin Mary—." This and a lot of other such examples got to Twain. He insisted he could see a "groveling spirit" in too much of this old art.

Personally, I don't see the groveling, which doesn't mean it isn't there. Twain's principle seems sound enough. If artists are groveling you should be able to see traces of it in their work. Maybe so. Anyway, I'm not interested in going on with the down side of this principle. I want to get to the up side. Charlie Russell never groveled, and it shows.

Russell wasn't painting patrons, and he wasn't painting for patrons. It was his wife's idea to start selling the pictures, and she handled all the business transactions. Lucky for him, she was good at what she did. So Charlie didn't have to dirty his hands with money. This kept them both happy and it kept Charlie independent and, oh Lord, was he ever independent. There's no trace of painting for money in any of his work.

Russell's self appointed mission in life was to record the old west, the land and people he loved so much and missed so dearly. He showed them as they were, exactly as they were, plains Indians with real features, horses, buffalo, cattle, grizzly bears in action, working and romping cowboys, and land with purple tints. Each picture was carefully selected from the memory bank to give the best feel (there's no other word will do) for how things were. And all this became our best, truest, and most reliable record of Montana in the old cowboy days.

But now is now. I have to stay with today. The real west is what the motorist sees. There's no point in getting too hung up on looking for the old days. They're gone. The cowboy bought himself a helicopter. The old fort is a prettied up registered historic site with outside parking and a Department of the Interior information counter inside. And the Indian is working on his masters degree in computer sciences. The old history is a closed chapter. It's fun to follow, and there are well kept places to see. But the real west is what we see as we drive along. It's our world now.

We work, raise families, vote, age, retire, drive around the country, and dream of grandchildren and paid up mortgages. Like the purple sage, our young dreams have been pushed off to the side of the road, or worse, into the gully. Comfort, crops, pensions, grandchildren, and good roads are enough for middle class dreams. But the purple sage sits along the sidce of the road, and in the gullies, like a quiet criticism. It keeps watch from the edges, poised, ready, waiting, a reminder of other times, other ways, open land, of people who loved the land as it was, Blackfeet, Sioux, Assinboin, Crow, fur traders, ranchers, and above all, of the big laughing cowboy who lived the dreams of his youth, saw the end of the open range, and drew honest pictures. Charlie's gone. Progress continues. I drive on. The pictures will never die, and the purple sage stays quietly on along the side of the road and in the gullies.

Chief Joseph's Campaign

The site of the last Indian battle in the United States, the Chief Joseph battlefield is about twenty miles south of Chinook, on a wide, nearly empty plain beside the Bear Paw Mountains. This is one of those small, barren, mountain clusters, thrown out here and there across central Montana in advance of the Rocky Mountains. It's easy to follow the details of the battle. The Department of the Interior has posted neat and easy to follow directions for the benefit of armchair generals and history buffs. So long as I'm giving credit, though, I also want to acknowledge for myself, and I'm sure for a lot of other travelers, that we owe someone in the state government a vote of thanks for doing a great statewide job. Montana's historic signs are superb, sometimes sad, sometimes very funny, and always clear and to the point. That's something I wanted to say before getting around to bad times and greed.

Tacitus, an ancient Roman historian, was reporting on the simple pastoral people of his time, the "barbarian" German tribes. The gods seemed to have denied them any deposits of silver or gold. Tacitus says he doesn't know whether the gods did this in mercy or wrath. It was mercy, Tacitus, pure mercy. Gold and silver were the worst of all curses. Any sensible Indian, given the choice, would abandon his own gods and worship at the altars of those old German gods. My maternal grandparents prospected out west back in the late 1800s, and I'll always remember them, and the friends who used to come and visit, as kindly old people. But the record is that prospecting greed was responsible for as much, or more, cruel treatment of Indians than anything else in American history.

The Nez Perce Indians of west central Idaho weren't hostile. They were our friends. They helped Lewis and Clark on their great trip of western exploration. They worked with fur traders and the army. They were allies. But none of this counted for anything when gold was found on their land. And it didn't matter either that the land was supposed to be protected under the terms of a treaty that they signed with the United States Government. Prospectors illegally invaded the land, and the army was moved in to protect the invaders. Then some United States Commissioners came along and insisted the Nez Perce Tribe had to sign a new treaty giving the land to the United States. One of the chiefs sarcastically remarked that the law abiding Nez Perce had to give up more land because the United States was intent on breaking its own laws. But that chief was a realist. He signed the new treaty. The problem came with some non-treaty Indians, people like Chief Joseph who refused to sign the treaty.

This was 1877, fairly late in our history. Indian wars were things of the past and, sensibly, Joseph's only choice was submission. The realists were right to sign the treaty and Joseph, the standout, was bitterly criticized by many in his day. The early western historian, Herbert Howe Bancroft, goes on and on about Joseph being an impractical religious dreamer, a liar, and a killer. But, on the other hand, Bancroft didn't seem to have much problem with what happened to the treaty Indians. Congress did the same thing it did on the previous treaty, it reneged on the amount of money it was supposed to pay. And, even at that, the Indians never saw the smaller amount of money it was supposed to pay. It disappeared. The Government agent said it was lost in a robbery. None of this sorry record, however, seems to have had a deciding influence on Joseph's actions. He had his own reasons.

Bancroft, although he doesn't accept them, gives these as Joseph's arguments for not signing the treaty, "——he steadily replied that the maker of the earth had not partitioned it off, and men should not. The earth was his mother, and, sacred to his affections, too precious to be sold." Joseph, evidently, was a religious visionary. Then we are told he was also deceitful. He deceived the army and commissioners every time he thought it would help his cause. And, when pressed with a final ultimatum, he started his long trek to this last battlefield by shooting some settlers.

The trek ended, after six days of battle and siege, on this lonely mountain plain. Chief Joseph surrendered, was sent as a prisoner to Fort Buford, and never again saw Idaho. But for the ten weeks leading up to this surrender, Joseph, along with about three hundred braves and their families, set an incredible record in fighting ability, courage, endurance, and suffering. They traveled a round about route of about two thousand miles, lived off the land, and either eluded or beat the army in every engagement. They were trying to make it to Canada. This is as far as they got. It's a quiet, brown, dry place with peaks in the distance. There's a plaque showing Chief Joseph, the victorious Colonel Miles, and Chief Joseph's sad words of defeat: "From where the sun now stands I will fight no more forever."

Captain Lewis and Miss Wood

I'm pleased with myself because I'm getting better at anticipating the geography. I took a little side trip down State Route 223 to pay respects at the Marias River. There were bluffs in the distance and I figured the river would be just below the bluffs. It was. I know the spotting of distinctive river bluffs, the water forced cuts of dry areas, is a fairly simple accomplishment. Still, it's fascinating to know, and see for myself, the shaping power of water. It's fascinating, too, to drive down the hill and find a river. It looks so cool and surprisingly welcome.

I spent about fifteen minutes walking around, mostly on the bridge. There's a road, some private property off to the left, and a small tank farm on the right. But none of this had an effect on the river. I didn't see any people or other cars. It was just me, a bridge, and the Marias River. To the west, there's a sand colored bluff on one side, and trees on the other. There are low banks, with autumn colored trees on both sides as the river flows east. And the clear calm water reflects every detail of the bluff and autumn colors. It's peaceful and beautiful, and that makes everything seem right.

The Judith River, which is about seventy miles southeast of here, was named for the woman who later married Captain William Clark. The Marias River was named for Miss Maria Wood of Albemarle County, Virginia, a woman who did not marry Captain Merriwether Lewis. I don't know why they didn't get married.

I don't think it had anything to do with them being cousins. Cousin marriage was acceptable in those days. Maybe she thought he was dead. That's one of the first things Lewis and Clark heard on their return. They were told that after an absence of more than two years, most people gave them up for dead. This, by the way, doesn't include President Jefferson. He held to his confidence in Captain Lewis. Anyway, there was no marriage, and I haven't been able to find out why. My guess is that Miss Wood never knew of Captain Lewis' feelings. I think he was shy with the back home ladies.

He was comfortable and in command in a man's world. The old portraits, sorry to say, are bland. He looks pleasant, but we don't see greatness in those round faced boyish features. And, personally, I think he looks uncomfortable in fancy dress clothes. But his own men, the Indians, and even the wilderness grizzly bears knew that he was smart, strong, direct, and forceful—a man to be respected. It's all in the journals that he and Clark composed on their great exploration of the west. It's manly and honest writing. I think the only artificial note in the whole thing is the entry on Miss Wood.

I'm not being critical of Captain Lewis. I just think he was shy with the ladies. Judging by the letters he wrote, he certainly liked to think about women. He'd ask his mother to give his regards to all the girls. He'd ask his friends to write about girls that might be available. He made no secret of it. He wanted to get married. But none of this was written to eligible young ladies. His feelings on these matters seem to have been expressed only to relatives, familiar friends, and his journal, which wasn't published until years after his death.

As I figure it, he was infatuated with Miss Wood, but it was a shy and distant infatuation. It's worshipping from afar when a young man says that comparison isn't worthy "with the pure celestial virtues and amiable qualifications of the lovely fair one." Miss Wood's name never came up again. Captain Lewis died tragically young, still unmarried. He left one legacy to a young lady, the name of a river.

Not seeing any flowers in the area, I took two yellow leafs from the side of the road and dropped them from the middle of the bridge. Respects Miss Wood. It's a long way from Albemarle County, but the Marias is a quiet and lovely river. Respects Captain Lewis. A grateful country will never forget your manly courage.

Glacier National Park and Marias Pass

The road needs repair; the glaciers are receding; and a few more signs would be nice. No road complaints from me, however, and I didn't hear any from other visitors. The road work is being done and will be completed very soon. You can see the glacial receding at the big 3D floor model at the visitor center on the Route 2 side of the park; and, again, at the roadside Jackson Glacier exhibit. It's nature and unpredictable, but that doesn't detract that much from the overall glory of the park. And let's hope that the Park Service will be able to divert funds to the sign shop after the roadwork is done. So now let's get on to the park itself, a wonderful slice of American real estate.

U. S. ROUTE 2 - CANADA TOO!

Where have you come from? Where have you been? Where are you going? Swapping stories with other tourists is half the fun of visiting national parks. I got a little tired of listening to the woman who kept talking about how incredibly smart her son is. I liked the fellow who was sharing my binoculars at a lookout point. None of the rest of us could agree, but he kept trying to convince his daughter that a tiny white spot near the top of the mountain was a mountain goat. Why wasn't there any movement? Well, he said, maybe it's sleeping. Anyway, so long as you don't mind not seeing goats, Glacier National Park is a nice place to meet other tourists.

I suspect the back packers out on those foot trails see mountain goats, moose, snakes, and whatever else is out there hiding from us noisy types. So long as they're hiking and packing, they've earned it. About all I saw was a couple of deer, and some loons on Lake McDonald. But I had a good time rolling along with the rest of the rowdy crowd. It's my usual choice. So far, incidentally, in driving Route 2, I've seen cattle, ducks, geese, two bald eagles, other birds I can't identify, fish, and occasional deer. I'm seeing what I want to see, and I'm comfortable with my limitations. In fairness, though, I think I should point out that, with about fifteen hundred square miles of park, and almost a thousand miles of foot trails, there's a lot of Glacier National Park I didn't see. With still more fairness, I'm happy to say the National Park Service built a road that's almost always open and is a visual and engineering wonder. Thanks to this, there's a lot of Glacier National Park that I did see.

And here again, by the way, we run into our old friend Theodore Roosevelt. He was a year out of office when this place became a National Park, but the action started while he was President. Teddy was a great supporter of the parks program. But just writing this makes me feel defensive. By now it must sound like Teddy is my hero and that's why he keeps showing up in these stories. Just to keep the record straight, I do admire Theodore Roosevelt, but my number one hero is George Washington. And I'm not putting Teddy anywhere, I'm just finding him. He put himself here, there, and everywhere across the map. He was the bully activist and, to give him the credit he deserves, he did know and sincerely love our land.

Also, before getting back to the park, I want to mention my own little nostalgic experience. About half way along, on the mountain road to the east entrance, I had some grand views of the plains. The geographic change is sudden, and the contrast, especially from a height, is startling. On my side it was all rock, hill, trees, green, and autumn. Down there it was level, brown, and gold. It still looked enticing and inviting. It was a nice view of the great plains before entering the world of mountain grandeur.

It's a land of massive shapes. There are great forests, and even greater mountains that soar above the tree line: steep mountains, gentle mountains, pointed mountains, rounded mountains, solid mountains, and mountains with crumbling rock debris. The rocks have different shades and colors. The hollows and valleys have sculptured shapes. There's still some year round ice and snow although, as noted earlier, it has receded in recent years. The lakes are mountain clear and pure. And that marvelous road runs from end to end. The engineering feat, and it's a little scary, is the long twisting way they got it along the sides of the mountains and down to the bottom of the valley. But it's safe and, with good overlooks, it's a comfortable way to see the wild and majestic beauty of this geologically complex corner of the northern Rockies. And now it's back to our regular road.

Route 2 runs along beside the Park. It follows along with the railroad through the last of the Rocky Mountain passes. Mountain men, people like Jim Bridger who led brigades of fur trappers through the mountains, found and exploited the passes south of here. The army, wagon trains, and railroads followed, and the national east-west traffic patterns were set. But not even Bridger was willing to spend much time up here. This was the land of the Blackfeet Indians, one of the most feared tribes in the west. Even the proud and ferocious Sioux could make occasional agreements with the advancing white civilization. The Blackfeet, as long as they were strong, didn't compromise. They would kill any outsider, white, Sioux, or Crow, found in their territory.

Eventually, of course, they gave ground. Mostly it was smallpox, and then there was the U. S. Army, and the usual irresistible white assumption. Anyway, by this time there was no one left who knew for sure of this last pass through the mountains. There were old stories, rumors, and, later on, someone found an earlier map indicating the location. But, prior to its modern discovery, no one knew, and no one paid any attention to the early evidence. The west was full of unsubstantiated old stories. Then too, there's nothing obvious about this pass as you approach it from the east. It's just mountains without any clear indication to show a relatively low grade passage.

There's an exciting story about how John F. Stevens, an engineering scout who worked for Jim Hill, found this, Marias Pass as it is now called, in 1889. He was alone, away from his base camp, and, with darkness closing in, he had to stay in the pass overnight without a fire. It was bitter cold, and he paced back and forth all night long to keep from freezing to death. The next morning he rode back to his base camp with news of a new passage through the Rockies. Jim Hill, fortune's favorite, had his own route west.

Everyone gets, and deserves, credit along this stretch of road. The Indian land begins just to the east of the pass. There's a big sign saying "Welcome to Blackfeet Nation." and, beside it, there's a stand with quietly courageous statues of two Blackfeet Braves. Then, at the pass, there's a highway pull-off with a statue of John F. Stevens, an oblisk honoring Theodore Roosevelt, and a plaque honoring William H. Morrison who was a local donor of land.

The only through route north of here is that engineering marvel in Glacier National Park. It's closed in winter. That's exposed country and the snows can run thirty and forty feet deep. Route 2, in Marias Pass, is the northernmost all weather route in the United States. It has its ups and downs. At different times its over, under, and beside the more nearly level railroad track. But, as anyone can readily see in driving along, it's in the pass. It's our northern road through the Rocky Mountains.

Kalispell Again

I like this town from the last time. We were traveling and, every time we came to a town, Terry had to visit the shoe stores. We would be going to a wedding when we got back to Maryland and she needed shoes to go with her blue dress. None of the other places had the shoes. However, when we got to Kalispell, she walked into the first shoe store she saw and found exactly the shoes she wanted. Oh boy, I said to myself, this is a town that has what it takes.

And it's set up to be comfortable and convenient for travelers. It has the standard highway cluster of motels and restaurants, most of them chain operated. I'm hooked on these places. They're predictable, moderately priced, and part of the life of the highway. They're full of fellow travelers, lots of people coming and going. Most of us give nods and friendly greetings—"Good morning," "Going far?"—and other such chit chat. It makes you feel part of the human flow, and it doesn't tie you down. We all hang loose so we can come and go as we please.

I know there are travel writers who are offended by places like this, especially when they find some of the restaurants are fast food places. They can carry on endlessly about their own feelings, and about how upset they were with familiar sights. They have refined standards and don't want to rub elbows with the rest of us in cheap restaurants. I expect it takes time for them to line up and describe their choice of restaurants and lodging, and then they spend some more time talking about the seasoning on the artichokes. By this time most cluster customers are off doing their own thing. Me, I'm enjoying Kalispell.

It's a Rocky Mountain valley, mountains on both sides and this nice little city in the middle. It's clean and well kept. Obviously, they have civic pride. The friendly Chamber of Commerce is a converted railroad depot, just down the street from a good pizza restaurant. The county building is stunning, good design, yellow bricks, and a location right where the road forks. I walked around it and took a couple of pictures, but I couldn't get a good close up vantage point. It's going to come out too big for my camera. But it sure is an impressive building, a mellow presence straddling and overlooking Main Street. On the east side of town, over around the historic Conrad Mansion, there's a residential sprinkling of mountain ash trees. They use these for decorative purposes and it looks nice. There are well kept lawns, soft green leafs, red berry clusters that grow out at this time of year, nice houses, some open fields, and mountains in the distance. It's really easy to find things to admire, things that are, in fact, beautiful in this town.

The elusive distinctive is usually more of a problem. But here it was like Terry's shoes. It didn't take much looking around. It's art. Downtown has several galleries. Drug store racks have sections given over to art magazines, popular and specialized, some I've never seen before. It's obviously a popular pastime. More than that, it's a professional calling. Just in walking around you can see some of the pictures in hotels, stores, and banks, and it doesn't take any special skill or training to spot quality. The real thing has a way of speaking for itself. It's here, strong, vibrant, saucy, serious, and happy, all true, and all western. Kalispell is a genuine western art center.

IDAHO

The Shape of the North

It doesn't look like Ohio, but it's the shape of Ohio politics. I don't know what it is with that state but they sure do turn out some tough politicians. They took the Toledo strip and Michigan had to settle for the Upper Peninsula. Out here it was a judge from Ohio, Sidney Edgerton, who arranged that run over border where Montana gained and Idaho lost. Look at any map of the area and you can see the size of what Idaho lost.

Back in the 1860s, when it was all Idaho Territory, Sidney, a former Congressman came out here with a Fededral appointment as Chief Justice. Idaho's Governor Wallace snubbed him. It seems the governor didn't care much for easterners. Sidney didn't care much for being snubbed, so he got busy and worked on carving out the Montana Territory. Idaho didn't object, or at least they didn't raise any objections until it was too late to change anything. They were willing to accept the division of the territory into two states, but they thought their border would be a straight line from south to north. What they didn't know is that Sidney was pulling strings with President Lincoln and members of Congress to get approval of that hiked-up border for Montana. To this day, Idaho is stuck with the results of his successful politicking.

It probably isn't fair to single Ohio out for blame. It's just that people from that state seemed to have an exceptionally keen sense of how to go about these things. Other people tried some of the same land grabbing games, but they weren't very good at it. Eugene Semple, for example, Washington State's last Territorial Governor, used to give

U. S. ROUTE 2 – CANADA TOO!

assurances that, of course, Washington would pick up this skinny part of northern Idaho. It would come, he said, as part of the statehood bill, and he was only saying what most people believed. There were some good reasons for combining this part of the state with Washington, but it didn't happen. Semple came from a family of Illinois politicians and he didn't know how to work these things. So he failed, but that's not a great disgrace. Except for the Ohio politicians, it seems that just about everyone failed in their early land schemes.

Idaho wanted to take over some non-Mormon parts of Utah. At one time they even suggested giving up this northern area in exchange for a part of Utah. Nevada tried to take some of Idaho's mining areas. Oregon was busy trying to get the Walla Walla valley away from Washington. Then there's this overall area called the Inland Empire, the mountain and inter-mountain regions of the north—this part of Idaho, the neighboring areas of Washington and Montana, and maybe even a pretty good cut of Oregon. Every so often someone tries to form this into a separate state, and the suggestion usually includes giving it a popular name like Columbia or Lincoln. In terms of the history and geography of this area this makes pretty good sense, but it requires more than this. They should try to get some help from Ohio.

Anyway, all I wanted to say is that I'm only seeing a narrow strip of Idaho. But what I am seeing is a scenic delight. Some historians say the state's name is a Shoshone Indian word meaning gem of the mountains. Sounds like a good descriptive name, but I'm not sure whether the gem is supposed to be the mountains, or what's in between the mountains. Personally, I like the in between. So far as I'm concerned the mountains are the rough setting, a rugged backdrop to show off the gem like quality of the valley.

I don't really think of mountains in these terms as I'm driving along. They're just mountains, so much scenery, sometimes pretty, and frequently impressive. But people don't live in, or on, the mountains. It's when I stop for a closer look that I realize what they really are. Shortly after you enter Idaho, there's a pull-off overlook to give motorists a good view of part of the Moyie River. Looking to the north you see a dam with the river backed up behind it. But that's in the distance. You can't look down and see the river in your immediate vicinity. There is another overlook up by the dam, a place where you can follow the course of the river as it leaves the dam. But that's not the same thing. Last time around I spent a little more than an hour poking around the side roads on my own. I'm impressed with the graceful strength of the underside superstructure of the Route 2 bridge over the river. Other than that, some open fields and sheep, there wasn't much to see. There's a hydroelectric site with an F.E.R.C. license number warning people that the area beyond isn't open to the general public. It's obviously a concern for safety, and I can see why. There's a tremendously deep chasm. But that was the attraction all along. I wanted to look down the chasm and see the river at the bottom. Instead I found an official looking warning sign. Another thing I've noticed is local advertising by outfitter companies. They provide equipment and guides. The mountains may be beautiful scenery, but they're not for casual poking around.

Inside is for loggers, hunters, survey teams, thrill seekers, and people who write strange articles for the Sunday papers, the suffering souls who go to the darndest and most impossible places and then write to tell the rest of us about how painful it was. If suffering is really good for the soul, these people can become canonized saints by wandering around in this country. They can get all sorts of scrapes, bruises, nosebleeds, broken bones and, depending on the time of year, bug bites or frost bite. They can get lost, wet, fall off cliffs, and have dangerous encounters with snakes, grizzly bears, and sure footed mountain goats who would just as soon butt them off the mountain. Teddy Roosevelt came out here to take a turn at doing most of these things. He fell off a cliff, brushed himself off, and then went limping off with the guide until he finally shot a mountain goat. But it took him three weeks because the goat didn't want to be shot, and, anyway, Teddy was only having his usual good time. His trip had nothing to do with the spiritual joy of pain and suffering, so I don't expect it did his soul much good. But that's enough of Idaho's wild mountains and chasms, real writers, a great president, and spiritual concerns. It's off to the valley for me.

The road follows big loops, and takes fantastic swings north and south; it follows to the end of mountain chains, goes around hills, and through occasional passes. Overall, though, it stays with the natural valley route. I love it.

Bonners Ferry

Bonners Ferry is a town that has the good fortune to be in the middle of all this scenery. It has a mid point location in the valley, highways in both directions, a good river, a beautiful wildlife refuge, and a used up supply of downtown parking spaces. It's a surprisingly busy place. I had to circle around a few times to find an open space. Maybe that's because the place is a little close and jumbled, still pretty much an old lumber town. But that just made it seem more friendly and cozy when I went strolling and window shopping after lunch. It's well kept, a comfortable walking place, and it's host to the Kootenai River and the Kootenai Wildlife Refuge, a good place to see the quiet natural beauty of the valley.

The Kootenai River is a sparkling and welcome visitor. It's a Canadian river that crosses to our side of the border, loops through parts of Montana and Idaho, and then flows back north to Canada. I've been enjoying its antics since Libby, Montana—a waterfall, rapids, and changes in appearance to reflect local surroundings. It's nice all along the way, and here, just about where it turns to return north, it slows to a wide sprawl around a good size reclaimed area. The Refuge is the open drained flood land between a big bend in the river, and the Selkirk Range of the Rocky Mountains. It's an ideal arrangement, wide expanses of water, marshland, grass, underbrush, and forested mountains, a perfect setting for the waterfowl, other birds, and little animals that call this place home. All of which makes the whole place natural—just natural, not wild. And this brings me back to something that happened many years ago when Terry and I were out here on a vacation trip.

During that earlier visit, a friendly lady ranger told us that all foot trails were closed, and, once in the park, we would have to stay in our car. It seemed there was a full grown persistent grizzly bear somewhere in the area. The poor thing had been caught twice before, banded with a radio collar that emits some kind of signal that can be picked up by monitoring equipment, and sent far across the Selkirk Range. But Mama Grizzly liked it jist fine here. She plodded her way back again and she had two cubs. The rangers caught the cubs. They were being held in outdoor cages and, because the holding area was laid with traps for mother, we weren't allowed to go in and look at the cubs. Absolutely not.

With houses in the area, and downtown Bonners Ferry just five miles down the road, we could see why the bear had to be caught and sent away again. It's common sense. Grizzly bears are the largest and, sometimes, the meanest animals in North America. They can stand over eight feet tall, and weigh well over a thousand pounds. No one wants that kind of critter for a neighbor. But, at the same time, we had to have sympathy for poor old Mama Bear. She was following a natural instinct, and this section, with its mountains and refuge areas, would have made a beautiful home range for the cubs.

No, said the nice lady ranger, she wasn't here at that earlier time and, although she knows there are grizzlys in the hills, there have been no problems with them in the park. With low rainfall it has been a bad year for berries in the mountains and so the black bears come down occasionally looking for food, and she saw a moose here the day before yesterday. But everything is under control and the local wildlife, mostly waterfowl, is doing just fine.

Sorry Mama Grizzly; sorry cubs. I can't think of anything I could have done or should have done—but I asked.

Sandpoint, Lake Pend Oreille and Priest Lake

The Sandpoint visitor's center is low profile and good taste. Looks like a wise investment in tourism, a good Route 2 location on the edge of town, an attractive building, ample parking, nice walks, and a view overlooking a wide creek. Full pamphlet racks inside, information counter, rest rooms, and a big three dimensional relief map showing locations of lakes, beaches, mountains, ski lodges, golf courses, and lodgings. Shame to come out with an uneasy feeling. It's a bright and cheery place, and the young people at the counter were full of friendly enthusiasm. I just took a couple of pamphlets, thanked them, and left.

I've decided that, this time, the problem isn't me. It's the visitor's center. With all those pamphlets and displays it gives the impression that this is a real resort area. It isn't. In fact it has a long way to go before it meets the idea of a real resort. It has lakefront development but it doesn't have high rise or condominium buildings blocking our view of the lake, and it doesn't have most of the rest of what goes with them. There are a few lodges that look like nice places, but that

U. S. ROUTE 2 - CANADA TOO!

isn't the same thing. They don't even seem to have social directors. Another thing, real resorts know how to put on airs and, so long as I'm at it, I think there's some kind of rising scale to these things. The more artificial the attractions, the snobbier the people. It has something to do with justifying higher rates. And crowding and clutter help profits too. It's just an economic thing that seems to grow when popular places compete for business. So far it hasn't caught on here.

There's a nice open town square with a park and fountain. First Avenue, down near the lake, is trying. It has a good line-up of stores, gift shops, and restaurants, and, at the end there's a renovated covered bridge. It's full coverage, but it's not enough to make the difference. And it is definitely not what you would consider high class resort. Prices are reasonable, and people are easy going and friendly. Even on my dress up night in a good restaurant, the waitress joked, told me about her own vacation, and said I should order the off season special becaue dessert was included in the cost of the meal. The whole place is small town friendly, and it still has a good part of the old lumber, trucking, and railroad business. It just doesn't have the feel of a real resort.

Don't get me wrong on this. Personally, I like the place just fine. I'm especially happy with the city beach that juts out into the lake. It's too late in the year for swimming so I had it pretty much to myself. There's a big grassy area with old trees, walks, and a playground in the center. I sat on a swing and watched the terns. I walked along the beach and enjoyed the good sand, and clean, clear water. There are mountains all around and, with the sun shining, it's pure pleasure to walk, sit, and look. But it's not real resort. I'm holding to that because I can't see where theis place has gone in for the development and sacrifices necessary to get real crowds.

Lake Pend Oreille is almost all natural empty shoreline. They don't even have finished roads through most of the area south of here. Sandpoint itself is a nice small city. There's some development here and in a few other places along the north shore—motels, lodges, marinas, and some high priced residential areas. It's modern and pleasant, with all the amenities, but, even in their settled areas, they don't come close to filling in the available lakefront space. Then, as the water disappears south through about forty miles of low rolling mountains, there's virtually nothing. It's just plain old natural surroundings, trees, hills, shore, and wide, clear, empty lake. And the development record is about the same or worse in other parts of this would be resort area.

The roads are good and, I guess if someone's into skiing, the slopes of the Selkirk Range are about as good as you can find. It's a beautiful scenic area, but, again, it's limited to normal lodges, ski lifts, and things like that. Not enough emphasis on the economic aspects of promotion and development. But that's just something I saw in passing. My real worst case example is Priest Lake, which is less than an hour's drive north of Sandpoint.

Back in the 1930s, when the WPA people came through and wrote up this area, they suggested that Priest Lake might be the most beautiful lake in Idaho. It's easy to see how people can hold to that opinion. It's a large lake nestled in a hollow space in the Selkirk Range, and it's surrounded by as thick a forest as I've ever seen. Some of it, as pointed out by local literature, is virgin growth, and there's an awesome thrill in standing back and looking at these great old trees. But the point is that the old WPA writer would feel right at home if he came back. After more than sixty years he wouldn't find that much change. The new roads are a help, and there's some development, but not that much; after a block a sign says "Dead End." The biggest real change he'd fund is that the trees have grown taller. This is a rustic place, some boat slips, picnic areas, and state parks. Again, on a personal basis, I enjoyed poking around, walking the shore, and exploring some bays, and it was nice finding tall western white pine trees. When I get all through, though, this place is like everything else I've seen in northern Idaho. I like it but, in fairness, I can not recommend it to real resort types.

My apologies to the friendly people of northern Idaho, and especially to the nice young people in the visitor's center. But I'm clear on the definition, and this place doesn't make it as a real resort. It isn't enough to have good reasonable accommodations, friendly restaurants, scenic mountains, superb ski slopes, deep western forests, virgin stands, nearby wilderness, wide rivers, broad valleys, open countryside, long clear lakes between mountains, first rate public beaches, boating, and high clean air. You still haven't met the terms of economic competition. No over charging, no clutter, no crowding, no social directors, no snobs—no real resort.

WASHINGTON

A Suggestion

Back in the 1850s, when you were first organizing as a Territory, you thought it would be nice to be named Columbia, like your great river. But that had drawbacks. In one sense Columbia means the whole nation and, anyway, as Kentucky's inconsistent Congressman Stanton pointed out, when he knocked out your request, we already had a District of Columbia. Besides, he wanted to have at least one state named after the father of the country.

So you didn't select the name, but you take great pride in it. It's especially respectful the way you have a silhouette of George Washington on your roadside signs. And now, from what I read in one of your newspapers, you are trying to develop a new state slogan.

You are a great state, and you were named after a great person. Personally, I think your slogan should be based on these obvious facts. So my suggestion, and it is given freely, is that your new state slogan be: "Washington: No Better Name—No Better Place." Or, since you're so good with the silhouette, maybe in place of the name, you could show the outline of the state with the silhouette super imposed on it.

Spokane

I couldn't get any Stoddard King poetry books. Three used book stores were out of them, and there's no point in asking to be put on a mailing list. When one comes in it will be set aside for a local customer. It's hard to believe there's still so much demand. It's well over a half a century since King died, and he wasn't a major literary figure. Great poetry can't be produced on a daily basis, which is the way he wrote. He ran a newspaper column in Spokane for about twenty years. Every day he'd fill it up with comments, tid bits from readers, and another new poem. They were just funny little verses about whatever struck his fancy that day, neckties, baseball, something in politics—whatever. I guess he's still popular in Spokane because he was a graceful writer who liked good natured fun.

I feel a little let down about not getting the books. Otherwise, it was a good errand. The people in the bookstores talked to me about local history, and I got to walk through a lot of older areas on the edge of downtown. I saw overhead railroad bridges, vagrants, warehouses, vacant lots, old buildings, double parked delivery trucks, insurance, printing, hardware, second hand furniture, used books, newspaper stands, magazine racks, and corner sandwich shops. Every major city has this, a behind the downtown section for business supplies and local needs. It tells its own story about what's up front.

In Spokane the old section seems to be a community, a place where local people know each other. There's a friendly feel to it. Some of the windows have plants and flowers. The magazine racks have all the sleaze, high-brow, and everything in between that anyone could ever want. There are newspapers from all around the country, and some from overseas cities. The sandwich was fair, the coffee was good, and one place had a long soda fountain, stools, and a sign advertising sundaes. It's not a showplace area. It shouldn't be. But it's nice to know downtown is supported by a comfortable fringe.

Incidentally, before I get to the details of downtown, there really is an Inland Empire. Spokane is its capitol. They've won me over to that. I think it's because it's a capitol without a government. It can't be official so it's jaunty. When I got into the downtown area I found it to be a place of gay and lively surroundings, and there's nothing original about my thinking this. Before I was even born there was a great poet who had the same thoughts.

The poet was Vachel Lindsay and, after he died, Sara Teasdale wrote a poem saying the years never tamed him, and he was the "gayest among the wise." These were true and loving words from an old flame. They didn't marry. They parted friends and Lindsay, the exciting and untamed troubadour of American poetry, went on to build a new life in Spokane. He did, by the way, meet and marry a lovely Spokane girl, but that's a later and different story. The attraction, at least in the beginning, was the city itself. The "gayest among the wise" liked the atmosphere of this place.

Considering the time and place, there shouldn't be any surprise in what followed. Lindsay and King became friends, and they even worked together. The untamed and the fun loving collaborated on a sarcastically funny poem about saxophones, and the curse of jazz music. The unusual thing is that it was written at the expense of Lindsay's generous host, the Davenport Hotel. Lindsay accepted their reduced rate hospitality, settled in, and complained about the downstairs music, none of which, of course, carried up to his luxury suite. It's just that he preferred sweet music. King joined in for the fun of it. And everyone else, hotel management included, was happy with the sarcasm because it was done with grace and wit.

All this, needless to say, is just my way of rummaging around. Nothing personal intended, Old stories and funny poems happen to be one way of getting to know something about Spokane. Another way, and it's right in the center of downtown, is to see the Davenport Hotel. Just don't expect to see any laughing poets while you're there. In spite of my old stories, the hotel is really about other things. It's about money and the show of wealth. It was built in the heyday of mine owners, processors, shippers, and railroad owners—the Inland Empire millionaires. It's all about what appealed to them and, fortunately, it's still here for the rest of us to see and enjoy. It's still active and busy, and every bit as plush as it ever was. In fact, it now has a special and well deserved recognition. The United States Government has put a plaque on the wall saying the lobby is an historic monument. It's because of the design and décor. It's a great show of an old western ideal—neat, quiet, reserved, self-confident opulence.

There's wealth and the show of wealth. This is one of those places where individuals could strike it rich in nearby mines and lumber, or, more often, in services to the landlocked Inland Empire. By way of looking at some local history, I went to Daniel Corbin's house. He was a fellow who built railroads from here to wherever there was lumber or mining. It's an Inland Empire millionaire's mansion from the last century, solid and spacious. The thing that surprised me, though, is that his ample house looked so modest in comparison to some of the estates that were further ujp the hill. However, when I drove up the hill, I was looking for something else, not estates. So this is just another instance of finding what I didn't expect. That's all right. So long as I'm here it's good to see estates too. It's also a reminder that I can't get away from money being a part of the history. It's a wealthy city and, from what I've read and seen, it seems to have had some pretty responsible rich people, the type who take an active civic interest, set aside land for parks, and things like that. There's an art museum on Corbin's estate. Good for them, all of them. But this isn't what I was looking for.

Lindsay proposed to his wife when they weree on an evening walk in Cliff Park. That's what I was looking for and found. It's about the size of a small city block, compact but neat. It's part of the high rock rim that encircles so much of Spokane. And that's another reason why I was looking, but I'm not going back into all that old business. It's just so much more of my musty poking around. However, so long as I'm on a tangent anyway, there's still another place I saw and don't want to spend too much time talking about, Mount Spokane. It's about twenty miles out of the city. In my opinion, the best part was a drive through rich farmland and a bright and clean forest to get there. After that it's all mountain road, well paved but narrow. In most places there isn't a guard rail, and it frequently looks like it's a sheer drop over the side. The long views are spectacular and, at the top, there's a plaque commemorating veterans from the World War. After that I did look around to see how many lakes could be seen in this part of Washington and nearby Idaho. Then I had to take the same road back to the bottom and, with twists and turns, it still seemed like I spent too much time on the drop off side of the road. It's a thrill. Let's get back to downtown.

The sleek young ducks were splashing, crowding, and bobbing up and down for my popcorn. Then the ungainly fat old duck worked his way into the water, paddled over to where I was standing on the bridge, cocked his head sideways, and looked up at me with one bleary orange eye. He wasn't begging, just telling me he was ready now. So the young ones got less. Every time the old timer's head turned up, I aimed more popcorn in his direction. I don't know why, but I owed it to him. Smart old bird.

I can't remember ever having seen a fat old bleary eyed duck before, and I don't want to speculate on what happens elsewhere when

U. S. ROUTE 2 -CANADA TOO!

the poor things get old. It's a time and place for cheerier thoughts. Ash trees line the walks and they have millions of soft yellow leaves. The old railroad clock tower stands tall, strong, straight, and alone. Grass and flowers have taken over where there used to be railroad tracks and a depot. The great intricate metal frame of the pavilion building curves up to a graceful circle. And there's a rainbow across the waterfalls. These—these and nearby shopping—are the gay and lively surroundings. This is the sort of thing that attracts people with artistic temperaments, people like Vachel Lindsay, and little girls with princess dreams. Hold on now because I have to jump from great poets and litle girls to an old curmudgeon.

In the early 1970s, Jim Hill's old railroad, the Burlington-Northern, gave up an island and some bordering land along the Spokane River. The area was converted to park and pavilion use for Spokane's Expo 74. This is what's known today as Riverfront Park, an area designed to attract and please large crowds. There's theater, open area, and other attractions in the pavilion. There are large grassy and landscaped spaces with bridges and nice walks. The most exciting part is the lower end of the island. The Spokane River is fast and furious over rapids, and there are waterfalls on both sides of the island. Way back when, the settlers would huddle on the island to avoid Indian attacks. Now everything is bridged and you can see a part of the falls on either side of the old Upper Falls Power Plant of the Washington Power Plant Company. On one side there's a suspension foot bridge and you can see the rapids of the main stream. The other side has a series of levels and you can follow the downward fall of the water. And then you can ride in a gondola and see the thundering Spokane Falls crashing over and down a steep rock face. The park is full of delights, noisy, quiet, artistic, calm, and exciting.

On the side that's not downtown, they've converted an old flour mill into artsy little shops and restaurants. It's fun to tour. But the busier development is the skywalk on the downtown side. Ten full city blocks are connected by second floor walkways. Obviously, it's a bad weather convenience for people who live here. For tourists like me, it's a fascinating maze with a different surprise around every corner, stores, open shopping areas, clothes, gifts, cards, books, paintings, pottery, bakery goods, restaurants, and coffee shops. Everything's bright, friendly, and clean. Between blocks you can look down on the traffic. Between buildings you can look down on courtyards, outdoor restaurants, sculptures, and whatever else there is to see. It's downtown with charm.

So now I'm a sentimental Inland Empire loyalist. But it's not just because Spokane has grown into a truly beautiful city. It's more the jaunty thing. The old section has flowers and plants in windows. Lindsay and King were free to be funny about the Davenport Hotel. And the old duck is doing just fine in Riverfront Park.

The Columbia Plateau and the Grand Coulee Dam

The mighty Columbia River comes out of Canada. It starts in a valley lake on the east side of the Selkirk Mountain Range. It goes north for about two hundred miles until it can get around the end of the Selkirk Range. At this point it goes to the other side of the mountain range and reverses direction. It streams south to Washington, south and west through Washington to the Oregon border, and then west to the Pacific Ocean. Other rivers join in along the route, the Kootenai River, after its swing through Montana and Idaho, returns north and joins the Columbia on the Canadian side of the border. The Spokane River joins it in the State of Washington. The Rocky Mountains pour out their excess waters, and, one by one, the streams and rivers work their way to the low roundabout downsloping route, the channel carved out by the Columbia River. One by one they join the Columbia River, and the rain and snow that came from the Pacific Ocean to the western slope of the Rocky Mountains returns to the Pacific Ocean. But, before returning to its ocean home, the flow of water has to get around the Columbia Plateau.

It's a stark contrast. The Columbia Plateau isn't at all like the mountains, valleys, and forests along most of the river's route. This is a large dry inland place between two mountain chains, the Rockies on the east, and the Cascade Mountains on the west. This is a plateau that sits high above and aloof from the Columbia River. It's a different land structure, a place with its own peculiar geology, and its own dry geography. As the geographers draw moisture lines, they draw a big oval one around this area, and fill it in with some contrasting color, usually yellow. It averages to less than ten inches of rainfall a year.

It's only about ninety miles from Spokane to the Grand Coulee Dam, but the driving is across the Columbia Plateau. In appearance and physical surroundings its like another world. You notice the first change as soon as you leave Spokane. There are no more trees. At first you are on a long flat plain, dry, but farm fields and cattle. The country gets drier and rougher shortly after you take a northbound route marked for the Grand Coulee Dam It is sparse desert country, scrub vegetation, scablands, dirt, buttes with strange shapes, and coulees. The base and shapes are lava, hot liquid rock that was forced out of the earth and hardened on the surface. The whole high Columbia Plateau is lava. Volcanoes erupted, the earth opened, time after time, age after age, and, layer by layer hot lava spewed and gurgled out and, to a height of about a mile covered an area of about two hundred square miles between the mountains. The Columbia Plateau is the world's greatest lava mass, and the dominant land feature of this area.

The high lava mass pushed the Columbia River into the big bend it still makes around the central part of the State of Washington. Then the glaciers came. For the most part, the Columbia Plateau wasn't covered by glaciers. They came up to the plateau and were higher than the plateau, but they didn't cover it. But it was the rushing waters, the melt and overflow that did much of the shaping job on this terrain. Floods washed away the soil cover and created the scablands. Rivers, great churning rivers that were larger than anything we have today, wore the wide deep gullies through the lava. These are the present day dry bed coulees of central Washington. And it is more than just long forgotten rivers that carved them out. The Columbia River, the same one we still see coming down from the Canadian Rockies, was the principal architect of the Grand Coulee.

The present dam is in about the same place as an ancient dam, an ice mass actually, butted up to the edge of the plateau. This ice mass worked its way down from the north and rose to such a level that it reached over the top and actually covered a part of the high Columbia Plateau. The river was trapped in its own valley. It couldn't get by the ice mass or the plateau. The water rose and formed a large deep lake. Finally, along the top, the water found a weak point in the plateau. Year by year the lake overflow worked and carved its way along the weak spot, and across the plateau. The Columbia River resumed its flow to the sea and, as the rushing waters kept pouring through, a channel, wide and deep, cut through the top of the plateau. Then, just a few thouisand years ago, the ice melted, the lake dropped, the Columbia River resumed its old big bend course around the base of the Columbia Plateau, and the high level river bed dried and became the Grand Coulee. Then the United States Government came along and built.

At the time the Grand Coulee Dam was the largest concrete structure ever built by man. It's not massive in terms of the surrounding geography, or the land history we've been reviewing. It couldn't be. Those things are elemental earth forces operating over geological time spans. That's a different scale. In human terms, though, the dam is a stupendous structure, and one of our better national success stories. We moved in, controlled the river, influenced the environment, and created new wealth. The dam is a central structure in a planned regional design to control the flow of water, provide irrigation for more than a million acres of fertile soil, and generate electric power for the cities and farms of the west. It's an inspiring thing to see, the Grand Coulee Dam with a back-up lake that stretches out for more than a hundred and fifty miles behind it. And the lake, as it should be, is named after Franklin Delano Roosevelt.

Anyone can learn all they want to know about the Grand Coulee Dam, its statistics, engineering details, and the overall regional plan, by going to the visitor's center, looking at the exhibits, watching the movie, reading some of the handouts, and then taking the guided tour of the area. The tour includes the center, pump generator plant, power plant, and several good views of the great cement spillway. The whole thing's well organized, impressive as can be, public, and well publicized. It is, and deserves to be, one of the best known tourist attractions in America, and I really did enjoy the tour. However, I'm going to leave it at that, and go back up the hill. I'm still following the older history.

From the top of the hill, up where the Grand Coulee begins, you can look down and see Lake Roosevelt. It looks small in the distance. I'm high up now, back near the top of the Columbia Plateau. The geography is easier to understand. It's no wonder the rivers, the Spokane as well as the Columbia, had to work out a course around the base of this great plateau. Imagining the geology still gives me some problems. It's not because of the view downhill, that part is easy enough. The idea of this mile high plateau being lava outpourings all the way from here to parts of Oregon and Idaho is just about beyond me. I can see it, but I can't picture all the outpourings. My imagination isn't that good. The scale is too big for me. On the other hand, though, I can get a mental picture of the ancient glacier and lake. I've studied the scene from the top of the dam as well as from up here. It's big but not too big. I can see what happened, and I can follow the course of the glacial river.

From here back to Route 2, a stretch of almost thirty miles, it's all Grand Coulee. There's a good road, and some flat dry land on either side of it. Otherwise, most of the Grand Coulee is taken up by Banks Lake. It's a man made lake. Water is pumped up from the dam, stored in this long coulee lake, pumped out at the other end, and piped to farm areas south of here. Once again, the old coulee is being used to carry a Columbia River overflow. Following the path of nature along this road is fascinating. It's also one of the most scenic drives in the west. The old glacial river did a deep and varied shaping job. There are high brown water sculptured bluffs all along both sides, and the lake is blue, clear, and beautiful. I'm riding along the floor of the Grand Coulee and there's not a cloud in the sky. Life is grand.

Happy Attractions and Some Shameful History

Crops are in. Leaves are falling. The early morning air is nippy. Soon it will be time to move indoors. Soon, very soon, tourists will have to leave for their own home. Mellow thoughts. But the season's not finished yet. There's still some warmth in the daytime sun. There's still time for outdoor work and play. It's time to check gutters, weather stripping, and furnace filters. Valley products still have to be picked and shipped to America's markets. Then, with the season's work finished, with travel coming to an end, there's still time to mix with the festive crowds at Leavenworth, walk the woods in a sweater, and cross the mountain at Steven's Pass. And, on the way, there's some of the grandest scenery in America.

Wshington doesn't have a structure. It has a series of structures. Each, in its own way, seems to be a textbook example of whatever it is. Different textbooks, of course, and this can give some conflict at the edges. That's where you see the show of brute power. The Columbia

Plateau gives way to the Columbia River, and the river gives way to the Cascade Mountains. Look down from the high lava plateau. You can see and sense the shaping force of the great river. Then, on the other side of Leavenworth, Route 2 enters the mountains through the Tumwater Canyon, an area of cliff walls and steep drops. The erosion's incredible. It's easy, and of course true, to say it's the edges and contrasts that make the scenery so thrilling. Yet, each part has its own individual attraction. Personally, and this is getting a little beyond Route 2, I like Puget Sound. But, put to a local test, I think these mountains might win a popularity contest.

The Cascade Mountains are the youngest, and probably the most protected and loved mountains in America. They're a gigantic, rolling, roadless wilderness, a wildlife preserve where animals can study the antics of local enthusiasts—artists, photographers, scientists, mountain climbers, skiers, campers, hikers, and day trippers. There's tremendous beauty, and there are fascinating combinations, contrasts, and changes. High volcanic peaks came up about a million years ago and added to the variety of an already interesting original mountain chain. There's year round snow on the higher elevations. Water is abundant on the Pacific side, and scarce on the eastern side. This gives each side a different character and ecology. But enough of geography and their wonderful Cascades. It's time to consider some shameful local history, and then we have to get back on the road.

There was a time when the British tried to claim all of what's now western Washington. They tried to get the Columbia River for a border. We would come to the end of the Columbia Plateau, then the river would be the boundary. Everything west through to the Pacific Ocean, and all the way south to the Oregon border, would be British. Each country had arguments to offer, and historians still like to discuss the technicalities. I won't go into that. Separate and apart from any legal arguments, the British deserved to lose. At least our early American arrivals tried to be decent. The British were immoral.

They wouldn't let Yankee traders have pants, breeches as they were called in those days. No one controlled the land, but Great Britain's Hudson Bay Company ran the only trading posts in the territory. According to them, no one else was allowed to do business with the Indians. Doing business with the Indians, of course, usually meant traveling through the forest to an Indian settlement. Breeches could get torn on that type of travel. So the rule in the Hudson Bay Company was that Americans couldn't buy breeches unless they turned in an old pair with a wear pattern from an acceptable occupation, farming for example. New breeches wouldn't be sold if the old ones had the type of rips and tears one gets from traveling through the forest. There's shame in this historic event. No one had any right to make our traders go without breeches. It's a tawdry episode in British history.

Now this whole part of the Columbia River valley is gloriously American, and filled with apple trees, millions of apple trees. It goes on for miles. The road goes high and you look down on orchards. It goes low and you drive past fields with row after long neat row of trees. It's an impressive sight, a great river, fields full of apple trees, and bare brown hills on both sides. On one side it's the bluffs of the Columbia Plateau. On the other side it's the dry eastern slope of the Cascade Mountains. The whole thing must be a dazzling sight in the Spring when the apple trees are covered with delicate white blossoms. But it's not Spring. It's late Autumn and I have to stay with the season.

The scenery is magnificent, and the season's great, especially here. But mellow is mellow, and I'm determined to let it go at that. No melancholy, not for me. The cure turned out to be spending time in Wenatchee, eating fresh apples, and seeing all the busy activity. I spent some time in the warehouse area watching boxes, all of them proudly announcing Washington State apples, rolling along the conveyor belts. And I saw trucks and freight cars lined up waiting to be filled. Must be a good crop year. Everyone's smiling and there are banners, flags, and traffic tie-ups along Main Street. Busniess towns are good for me. The next place is a tourist town.

Leavenworth is—or isn't—what it is. I liked being with the crowds, and there's a nice success story here. But the place isn't really German, it only looks that way. Sometime, back in the middle of the last century, when the sawmill went out of business, the town had two choices, fold up or find a new business. By 1976 they had bounced back so far that Look Magazine selected them for an All American City award. The whole place was being changed into a Bavarian village. Their own citizens committee had decided that, as long as they were in an Alpine-like mountain setting anyway, they might as well turn it into the type of tourist attraction that's found in the

Bavarian Alps. Now it's complete, and a good colorful gingerbread job of make believe. Everything looks picture book German. Crowds are milling around the park, admiring the ornate bandstand, and visiting the outdoor stands to see what local artists are offering. Stores are featuring well made and pricey German clocks and music boxes. Jolly schmaltzy music is coming from recessed speakers. Restaurant menus include a good variety of German food and beverages. People are walking in all directions, visiting the attractions, and joining in the holiday atmosphere. It's a rousing success.

My own quiet success came in Stevens Pass. I got so absorbed with poking around in the woods, looking for railroad tunnels, and talking to people, that I forgot all about other feelings. The pass, incidentally, is just a good direct way to get from one side of the mountains to the other, and there are some nice scenic views. What I was looking for was the scene of a 1910 railroad accident. An avalanche buried a passsenger train and killed 118 people. Terrible thing. What I found, besides the scene of the accident, is Cascade forest and friendly people. I stopped for coffee and help with directions. The counter lady asked the short order cook to help me. He quit cleaning the grills, and tried to help me. But he got distracted with the details of my travel and we wound up matching notes on Idaho. Then a policeman joined in. He knew the details on all the tunnels, and he gave very good directions. I found the fatal hillside; it just looked like any other hillside. Here and everywhere else along the road, the best thing about travel is the people I meet.

End of the Road

There's a low bridge across the Snohomish River. Mile markers are reading down, three, two, one. There's a sign saying Everett city limits. Then I had three choices, north or south on Route 5, or Hewitt Avenue into Everett. I took the Hewett Avenue exit, went down a ramp, and followed an arrow which directed Route 2 traffic to turn left. Then I was on a city street with no more Route 2 signs. I found a policeman and asked what happened to Route 2. He thought it over and said, "It kind of dissolves. Where do you want to go?" I told him I was trying to follow Route 2 to the end. He looked a little surprised. Then he laughed and said, "Congratulations, you made it." That was my entry into Everett. Now I'm going to digress.

Before going on about myself and the city, I want to pay respects. It has been several years since the sudden and unexpected death of Senator Henry M. Jackson, who came from Everett. He started with the New Deal, and never lost his concern for the ordinary people of America and the world. I'm not here to eulogize. I just want to pay my simple respects. He was a good man who stood for American strength and idealism. I'm sorry he's gone.

So far as my own travel is concerned, it's over, and I'm ready to go home. No more feelings of regret about the trip ending. Actually, I only had a couple of odd days, not bad days, just days when I tried not to think about it. Sometimes I'm a little slow in swinging around to a changed mood. Besides, it's normal to have regrets about the ending of a good journey. It's normal, too, once I've accepted the change to start getting excited about a return to home and family. And Everett adds to the current mood. I don't think I've everr seen a city that's more home town America.

It has ships in the harbor, tree lined strets, clean neighborhoods, factories, and shopping centers. Every day at noon, the Trinity Lutheran Church chimes out with "Rock of Ages." Clark Park has big old horse chestnut trees. The whole place is homey, and the season is exhilarating. It's getting cooler, and there's a salt breeze. Everyone's wearing jackets. Downtown business is brisk and busy. I smelled fresh baked goods as I walked by a couple of shops and I started to wonder where we will have Thanksgiving dinner. It's up to the kids, but I hope they decide on my house. Now it's more than just mood, the season, and this home style city. It's time for me to go home.

Route 2 brought me to a good ending. The Cascades are clear, and close enough so I can see snow on some tops. The city has geography, geology, a river, a bay, ships, railroads, lumber mills, factories, stores, children, schools, churches, good people, and nice homes. It has the history, experience, and feel of America. George Vancouver, the original British explorer of Puget Sound, landed here in 1792. Jim Hill and John D. Rockefeller, along with various bankers, mine owners, and old lumber barons, built, invested, and finagled here. Working people, reformers, and radicals, organized, met here, fought, and struggled for the rights of labor. Lumber was shipped from here to build California's great cities. War materials were shipped from here. Airplanes were made here. It's a good brawny American working city, and it's a good comfortable home town.

The houses are on a hill. Actually, it's a high flat plateau between the river and the bay. The railroad and industrial plants are at the bottom of the hill, on a long narrow strip of land beside the water. It's a neat arrangement, and it's easy to see how the town evolved. Some of the old close worker homes are still occupied, and well kept, along Grand Park Avenue. Live up here where the air is cleaner, and the views are good, and walk down the hill to your job. I would guess that some of the people in this older part of town are still living that way. Basic conditions are still the same. And the plateau's all filled up now with houses, parks, schools, and churches. The whole place appeals to me as home town America.

It's nice. That's all, and that's enough. Some well to do homes, but nothing spectacular. It's a city of homes, well kept ordinary homes. Street after street of nice family homes, churches, and parks sitting on a high plateau that overlooks a bay of Puget Sound. I ended the trip with a stroll along a pleasant park that commemorates George Vancouver's landing. There are pleasant looking homes across the street. On this side we have grass, walks, flowers, benches, and an American flag. All's well.

Now I'm going back home to New Carrollton, family, and Thanksgiving. What I found is what Walt Whitman told me in the beginning. America is "Earth's modern wonder." Still true, Walt, still true.